EX-Z

"Saved by the Bell" titles include:

Mark-Paul Gosselaar: Ultimate Gold
Mario Lopez: High-Voltage Star
Behind the Scenes at "Saved by the Bell"
Beauty and Fitness with "Saved by the Bell"
Dustin Diamond: Teen Star
The "Saved by the Bell" Date Book

Hot fiction titles:

EX-ZACK-LY

by Beth Cruise

ALADDIN PAPERBACKS

Photograph and logo copyright © 1995 by National Broadcasting
Company, Inc. All rights reserved. *Saved by the Bell*™ is a trademark of
the National Broadcasting Company, Inc. Used under license.
Text copyright © 1995 by Aladdin Paperbacks
All rights reserved, including the right of reproduction
in whole or in part in any form
Aladdin Paperbacks
An imprint of Simon & Schuster
Children's Publishing Division
1230 Avenue of the Americas
New York, NY 10020
First Aladdin Paperbacks edition December 1995
Printed and bound in the United States of America
10 9 8 7 6 5 4 3 2 1
Library of Congress Cataloging-in-Publication Data
Cruise, Beth.
Ex-Zack-ly / by Beth Cruise.—1st Aladdin Paperbacks ed.
p. cm.—(Saved by the bell ; #22)
Summary: After lightning strikes Bayside High, the "Saved by the Bell"
gang raises money for new computers for the school by holding a carnival.
ISBN 0-689-80211-0
[1. Computers—Fiction. 2. High schools—Fiction. 3. Schools—
Fiction. 4. Carnivals—Fiction.] I. Title. II. Series.
PZ7.C88827Et 1995
[Fic]—dc20   95-20844

**To everyone who
likes to kiss**

Chapter 1

▲　▼　▲　▼　▲

The weatherman had been way off, Zack Morris decided as he peered through the rain cascading down the windshield of his classic '65 Mustang. The forecast had promised the perfect night for romance: a bright full moon, a gazillion stars in the heavens, and a dulcet ocean breeze.

The forecaster had barely drawled that the temperature would be in the low eighties before Zack had palmed the phone and punched in Kelly Kapowski's number. Kelly was not only the most beautiful girl at Bayside High, she was also the nicest and Zack's steady.

Zack had suggested they share an early romantic picnic dinner because he expected a major traffic jam on Lovers' Lane once night fell. The road led out of Palisades along the seashore. It was even more picturesque than California Highway One and was the most popular spot for sweethearts to snuggle while enjoying the scenery.

Now that it was pouring rain, there wasn't much to see in the way of scenery, but, since they'd moved their picnic inside the car, there was definitely a lot of time for him to snuggle with Kelly.

Zack draped his arm along the seat behind Kelly and leaned closer to her.

Kelly glanced up at him. "Still hungry?" she asked. "I think there's a couple of buffalo wings left in the bucket, but we're all out of extra sauce for dipping."

Rather than have his girl in his arms, Zack found himself cuddling a box of leftovers.

"Actually," he said, setting the takeout container on the backseat, "I was thinking more along the lines of dessert."

Kelly licked barbecue sauce off her fingers. "Mmm," she murmured.

Zack moved closer again.

"What did you get?" Kelly asked. "Apple turnovers? Cherry tarts? Oh, not those to-die-for chocolate ladyfingers! I love those!"

"I wasn't thinking about food for dessert," Zack said. He caressed the tip of her chin, his touch urging her to tilt her lips up to his. "I thought a kiss would taste sweet about now."

Kelly's long eyelashes swept down and up again as she gave him a flirtatious look. "No pastries?"

"Not even peach cobbler," he murmured, and brushed his lips against hers.

"Mmm," Kelly said as she kissed him back.

Zack's heart swelled happily. After all the time he'd spent trying to worm his way back into her affections, he was exactly where he belonged. Although he'd planned for a moon-drenched, rather than rain-drenched, evening, just being alone with Kelly on Lovers' Lane was paradise as far as he was concerned.

"Mmm," Kelly whispered again. "I adore peach cobbler." She sat back in her seat, moving out of the circle of Zack's arms. "Did you know that we've got yogurt that tastes just like it at Yogurt 4-U? I thought it would be gross, but it is so good. I pig out on it whenever I have a break."

Briefly Zack wished that Kelly had never taken her after-school job at the yogurt stand. Or at least had never indulged in the dessert.

Kelly leaned forward to peer at the sky. The clouds blanketed every one of the gazillion stars Zack had counted on to set a romantic mood. "This is really weird, isn't it?" Kelly said. "An hour ago there wasn't a cloud in the sky."

"Real freaky," Zack agreed, thinking more about the kiss they'd just shared than about the weather. Everything had been going great, she'd been kissing him back, and then—whammo—she'd started talking about yogurt. Either the storm was affecting Kelly strangely, or he was losing his touch. It had to be the storm!

Zack glared at the rain as it lashed against the windows. It bounced off the hastily raised roof of his convertible with enough force to poke a hole in the fabric.

"You know," Kelly said, "this downpour reminds me of all those storms we had when we were in junior high."

Zack ran a hand back through his blond hair and wondered if he should attempt to kiss her again. Kissing had been the main event on his agenda for the evening, after all.

"Not exactly," he said. "Wasn't there a lot of thunder and lightning with those storms?"

"Was there ever!" Kelly agreed. "Remember how Mrs. Pendergast, our English teacher, decided it was perfect weather to read about Rip van Winkle?"

"Oh yeah. Didn't she say something about thunder being nothing but midgets bowling in the clouds?"

"I don't remember midgets, exactly," Kelly said. "But I do remember that you wanted to know if they were Bowling for Bucks."

As if making a comment, and not a nice one,

about Zack's questioning mind, the wind picked up. The rain rattled noisily against the car as the Mustang seemed to shiver when a strong gust buffeted it.

Kelly shivered a bit, too, and moved closer to Zack. "It's getting worse," she said. "Maybe we'd better go home."

"I would if I could see to drive," Zack offered, "but at the moment I think we're safer if we stay right where we are."

"Oh," she mumbled quietly and rather uneasily. "At least there isn't any thunder or lightning."

Suddenly there was a flash of light followed by a loud crack of thunder. With a squeak of fright, Kelly jumped into Zack's arms.

The situation would have been great, he decided, if it weren't for one small problem. He was getting kind of scared himself.

With the rain lashing against the windows, the wind rocking the car back and forth, the lightning nearly blinding them, and the thunder pounding louder than a heavy-metal rock band, even the most romantic guy in the world would have had trouble concentrating.

Kelly might be clinging to him, but Zack was clutching her just as tight, and he'd forgotten all about kissing.

"I sure hope it stops soon," Kelly murmured, her voice tight with fear.

"Me, too," Zack said with heartfelt emotion.

Off in the direction of Palisades a particularly bright zap of lightning zigzagged from the sky, aimed directly at a target in the city. The thunder exploded. With a yelp of terror, Zack and Kelly clung together even tighter.

"Whoa!" Zack muttered. "Was that ever a bad one!"

"Do you think it hit something?" Kelly asked.

Zack shrugged, suddenly feeling foolish for shirking from the storm. He sat up and peered off toward town. "If it did, I'll bet the damage is in the mega category. That was a whopper of a bolt."

Kelly slid back into her seat. "Well, it sure looks like it was the big finale," she said.

She was right, Zack realized. Only soft flickers of lightning lit up the clouds now, and the thunder had retreated. The wind had dropped, and even the rain was letting up. While he stared at the clouds, they parted, and soft moonlight spilled through the hole.

"Oh, look," Kelly said with a sigh. "I can see some stars."

As quickly as it had sprung up, the freak storm was fading away.

Kelly snuggled close to Zack. "Now, what were we talking about before Mother Nature distracted us?" she asked softly.

"Dessert," he said.

"Ah yes," she breathed, and tilted her face up, waiting for him to kiss her again. "Did you have any further ideas about it?"

"Sure did," Zack said. He gently caressed her cheek as he sweetly kissed her mouth. "Do you mind if I have seconds?"

"Not at all," Kelly replied.

Neither of them noticed the now moonlit night or the gazillion stars.

▲　▼　▲

The next morning when the alarm went off, Zack hit it and drifted back to sleep. If his mother hadn't called him, he would have missed seeing firsthand the disaster at school. As it was, he skidded to a stop at the rear of the crowd that fanned out around the doorway of the Bayside computer lab.

An unpleasant smell hung in the air, sort of like a combination of melting rubber, burning hair, and Mr. Belding's famous tuna casserole.

Zack wrinkled his nose and pushed through the mass of students until he reached the front of the crowd. Samuel "Screech" Powers was there, his curly hair looking wilder than usual, his soft brown eyes nearly bugging out.

Zack poked his friend in the ribs. "What happened?"

"A calamity," Screech said, his voice flat with shock. "Mr. Monza told us lightning hit the school last night."

"All right!" Zack shouted enthusiastically. "Was it that mega bolt?"

Screech groaned. "Yes," he said, now sounding as if he were in pain. "When Mr. Hayes opened the door this morning, he nearly cried."

Zack sympathized. He'd felt that way about going to school some days. Usually ones when he had a major test to live through.

"Really? Mr. Hayes cried?" Zack demanded.

"Well, his eyes got all watery. Ms. McCracken thought he was being sensitive and giving in to his emotions, but it could have been the cloud of smoke that billowed into the hall and engulfed him that did it," Screech admitted.

"So what smells so bad?" Zack asked.

Screech moaned. "The computers. I'm worried about Hillary."

"Hillary?"

"My favorite computer," Screech said, his voice breaking sorrowfully. He twisted a baseball cap between his hands, wringing it as he worried. "We're so close," he mumbled, and sniffed.

Zack dropped a hand on his friend's quivering shoulder. "I'm sure they're doing everything they can for her . . . er, it . . . er, Hillary."

"I know," Screech murmured tragically. "I have to trust Mr. Monza to pull her through."

Zack's eyebrows rose in surprise. Ever since Screech had inadvertently coated the home-ec room in melted marshmallow goop, he and Mr. Monza, the head of maintenance at Bayside, had tried to avoid each other. Zack certainly never expected to see Screech waiting anxiously for the man who considered his dorky buddy the human equivalent of a pesky stone in his shoe.

"And if he can't"—Screech took time out to blow his nose loudly—"well, at least Mr. Belding will be with her at the end."

There was a ripple of anticipation in the crowd as footsteps echoed inside the computer lab. A moment later Mr. Belding, the principal, appeared in the doorway.

"Hillary?" Screech asked.

"Suzette?" the tremulous voice of another computer geek murmured.

"Irma?" a third whispered.

"Frederick?" one of the girls demanded tearfully.

Mr. Belding raised his hands. "They're all . . . well, hanging on by a microchip," he said. "We lost some but, with any luck, the majority will pull through."

Nanny Parker wiggled through the press of concerned students. A pencil in one hand and a pad of paper in the other, she elbowed aside one last student until she was practically standing on the principal's toes. "Parker of the *Bayside Beacon*, sir," she said smartly. "We understand it was a power surge that caused the damage. Does this mean that surge protectors weren't utilized in the lab?"

"Of course they were," Mr. Belding insisted. "But a direct lightning strike of this size—"

"Were these surge panels state-of-the-art or a bargain variety chosen by the school board in a nefarious plot to undercut the quality of education in the school system?" Nanny snapped.

Screech gasped, as did many of the other concerned computer users.

"Don't be ridiculous," Mr. Belding said. "The equipment we use is—"

"Then it was because of carelessness on the part of unnamed persons that this happened? I believe there is supposed to be a lightning rod that is supposed to prevent occurrences such as this. Was it actually in place?" Nanny demanded. "Or was it mysteriously missing as it is this morning?"

Angry grumbling could be heard in the crowd of students.

"Yes, we did have a lightning rod," Mr. Belding admitted.

"*Did!*" Nanny shouted, latching on to the word. "And why don't we have one now?"

"Because it melted," the principal said.

Nanny wilted at the news.

"Melted?" Screech squeaked.

"Part of it did," Mr. Belding said. "Part of it

shattered, part of it twisted, and part of it just plain broke off. It did what it was supposed to do and saved the building from being hit—an event, I'd like to point out, which would probably have resulted in the school burning to the ground."

A new murmur echoed in the hall, one that sounded suspiciously like disappointment.

"The lightning rod gave its life for us," Screech murmured, and shook his head sadly.

Zack eased his way out of the crowd and tiptoed away from the mourners. He'd barely rounded the corner before running smack into Jessie Spano, Lisa Turtle, and A. C. Slater.

"Ew," Lisa said, wrinkling up her cute little nose. "If that's lunch I smell cooking, I think I'll pass on Ms. Meadows's special today."

"If that's lunch, we're having circuit-board surprise," Slater said, sniffing the air. "What is it exactly, preppie?"

"Well, it depends on who you ask," Zack admitted. "It's either Hillary and friends or the computer lab. Which actually comes down to the same thing. The lightning last night did a real number on dear old Bayside."

"The lab!" Jessie gasped. "Oh, golly! The equipment is all right, isn't it?"

"Depends on Mr. Monza's findings. He's the surgeon in charge at the moment," Zack said. "As I see it, the storm just gave me a free period this morning."

"A what?" Lisa asked.

Zack grinned widely. "From the smell of things, I'd say computer classes are canceled today. See ya!"

Chapter 2

▲ ▼ ▲ ▼ ▲

Jessie, Lisa, and Slater stared after him as Zack sauntered down the hall.

"Do you believe that?" Jessie fumed.

"With that gross smell nearly gagging me?" Lisa demanded. "You better believe it. The lightning must have really fried things good."

"I mean Zack," Jessie insisted. "How can he be so happy about a major disaster?"

"He gets out of class," Slater pointed out. "Hey! So do I, for that matter." He grinned widely, his dimples deeply creasing his cheeks.

"Oh, me, too!" Lisa cried happily. "Now I'll have time to change my nail polish. Do you believe this?" She held one hand up for her friends' consideration. "Isn't this color a total nightmare? It does nothing for my skin tone."

Jessie glared at them both. "What is this? An epidemic? Are all of you so blind? What happened to the computer lab is a catastrophe!"

Screech dragged down the corridor toward them, his long, thin face looking even longer and a bit haggard.

"Well, here's someone who will agree with you on that," Slater offered. "What's the latest, Screech?"

Tears brightened Screech's eyes when he glanced up at his friends. Manfully, he blinked them back. "It's Hillary," he said, his voice breaking worse than usual over the computer's name. "I don't think she's going to make it. Mr. Monza let me visit her, and it was . . . it was . . ." With a gasping sob, he turned hastily to bury his face on the nearest shoulder, which happened to be Jessie's.

She patted his back in a soothing manner. "Take it easy, Screech. If anyone can pull her through, it's Mr. Monza. What he doesn't know about fixing computers doesn't need to be known."

Slater's eyes widened. "Really? Then why isn't he making mega bucks in the repair business? Why is he pushing brooms at Bayside?"

"He doesn't push a broom," Jessie pointed out. "He has employees who do that."

"As head of maintenance, he is in a management position," Lisa agreed. "But actually, I think he stays here for an entirely different reason."

"Loyalty to Bayside," Jessie said.

"No."

"Variety of work situations?"

"No."

"Big bucks?" Slater asked.

"No!"

Jessie continued patting Screech's back, although his sobs were subsiding. "Then what is it?"

"His city pension," Lisa said. "We've been studying about them in my Life Is a Science class. Last week we learned about real estate, and let me tell you . . ."

Slater put his hand over her mouth, gagging Lisa before she could go into more detail. "Next thing we know, you'll be trying to sell us insurance," he murmured.

Lisa dragged his hand away. "That's next week's topic," she said.

Slater groaned dramatically.

The sound drew Screech out of his private misery. He straightened, knuckling away the remaining tears with his fists. "You had a favorite among them, too, didn't you, Slater. Which terminal was it?"

Since Jessie was glaring at him, obviously insistent that he humor their distraught friend, Slater donned a serious expression and sighed forlornly. "It's true," he said. "I didn't want anyone to know. Jocks aren't supposed to be sentimental about their computers."

"Just their footballs," Jessie mumbled under her

breath. Although she was proud of Slater's prowess in sports, that he was captain of both the wrestling and football teams, she rarely showed it.

"However," Slater continued, "there is a particularly cute little PC I've become very close to this last year."

"What's her name?" Screech asked.

Slater looked trapped for a moment. "Er, name? Well, it's . . . it's . . ."

"Oh, you know Slater," Jessie said, coming to his rescue. "He prefers pet names to real names."

"Right," Lisa declared, jumping in as well. "He calls Zack *preppie* and Jessie *momma*, doesn't he?"

Screech nodded thoughtfully.

"So, of course, I don't know my favorite terminal's *real* name," Slater said. "And, since it's a pretty personal thing, you understand that I don't care to share my private one with you."

"But I've overheard him talking to her," Jessie said, "and he calls her his cute little circuit breaker."

Slater's jaw almost dropped open.

Screech, however, got all sentimental. "I know how you feel," he murmured quietly. "Hillary is my cute little circuit breaker, too."

When his eyes got watery again, Lisa hastily searched her purse for tissues and handed him one.

▲   ▼   ▲

It was the next day before the full extent of the damage was known. Mr. Belding called a schoolwide assembly to give the students the bad news.

The gang scrambled to get seats together in the auditorium and were soon squashed shoulder to shoulder as the crowd swelled with concerned students and teachers. Jessie, Screech, and Lisa grabbed seats in one row while Slater, Kelly, and Zack took the chairs behind them. To get comfortable, and stake his claim on her, Zack draped his arm over the back of Kelly's seat. She might have agreed to go steady with him, but other guys were just predatory enough when it came to great-looking girls. If a guy didn't mark his territory, they'd try to steal his girl away.

Fortunately, Kelly didn't suspect him of such blatantly chauvinistic behavior. She smiled brightly at him as Mr. Belding took the stage.

The principal was wearing a black suit, as if in mourning. Since word had already leaked out that some of the computer terminals were so badly damaged that they were on their way to computer heaven, all the computer geeks were in mourning, too, sporting black armbands in remembrance.

Mr. Belding tapped at the microphone to make sure it was working. Then he squared his shoulders and cleared his throat. "Thank you all for coming," he said. "I know that a good number of you have been very concerned about the status of our computer lab. And I'm pleased to say I have good news. While damage was severe, Mr. Monza tells me that we lost very few of the patients. Considering the intensity of the lightning strike, we were very lucky in this. Repairs are in progress even as we speak."

The crowd rose to its feet with a shout of joy and a few tears of happiness as well. When Screech's bottom lip began quivering, Lisa pressed a handful of tissues into his palm.

"Settle down," Mr. Belding urged, his hands spread wide. "I also have some bad news."

As one, everyone dropped back into their seats.

"Uh-oh," Slater murmured.

Lisa scrambled to find more tissues, sure that Screech would collapse soon. She angled closer to him in her chair, noticing that Jessie did so on his other side, each of the girls determined to hold Screech up if his backbone turned too rubbery to support him.

Behind them, Zack leaned forward to put his hand on Screech's shoulder in a show of moral support. "Hang on," he whispered. "Remember, we already know Hillary is among the living."

"Unfortunately," Mr. Belding told the assembly, "the school budget doesn't allow us to accomplish all the major repairs and replacements until next year. Mr. Monza assures me that he and Mr. Hayes will be working diligently to get the lab back in working order, but we are being forced to cancel all computer-related classes for the rest of this school year."

Zack started to jump out of his seat in pleasure but subsided quickly when he caught Kelly and

Jessie glaring at him. The shout of joy died in his throat, hastily covered by a cough as he slumped back in his chair.

"Everyone taking a computer class will be gaining a new study hall," Mr. Belding announced, "so report to the cafeteria instead of the lab that period. Does anyone have any questions?"

Nanny Parker leaped to her feet in the front row, pencil and pad at the ready, and fired the first query. The rest of the assembly ignored her, and the principal's answers, and whispered among themselves.

"This is terrible!" Jessie hissed to her friends. "What does the school board expect us to do without computers?"

"Nap in study hall?" Zack suggested.

"It's sure what I'm planning," Slater said.

He and Zack exchanged a grin and a high five.

"What will you do, Screech?" Kelly asked.

Screech sighed softly. "The same thing I do in the evening and on weekends. Work with my PC at home. Actually it has more updated features than Hillary or her sister terminals had here." His mobile face scrunched up in sorrow. "*Had!* Oh, Hillary!" he sobbed.

The gang waited patiently while he blew his nose and took a ragged, deep breath to control himself. "Most of the other computer nerds have better hardware and more software at home, too," Screech continued. "It was affection that drew us to the old-fashioned system in the lab. This is where it all began for us." He sniffed again nostalgically.

"My home system isn't as elaborate as yours is," Jessie admitted, "but it is more functional than the computers at school have been."

"So the lab is no loss, right?" Zack demanded.

"For some," Kelly said. "But I don't have a computer to myself at home. I share it with six siblings and my parents. Between Mom's budget balancing, Dad's financial planning, Kirby, Kyle, and Kerry's college research papers, Nicki and Erin's computer games, and Billy's preschool learning programs, there isn't much disk space, much less time, available for me to use our home PC."

"Which just goes to show that we need to do something to get the lab working *this* year," Jessie declared. "If not for students who don't have PCs at home, then for a more important reason."

"Which is?" Slater asked.

Jessie shook her head sadly. "You Neanderthals aren't thinking clearly. If you ever do. Let me put it this way. Do you want to graduate this year?"

Slater frowned. "What do you mean *want to*?"

"We need a certain number of credits to graduate, don't we?" Jessie asked. "And we have to pass certain classes to even qualify for graduation, right?"

"You mean like English?" Zack said.

"And government," Kelly added.

"Phys ed," Slater contributed.

"Math," Lisa said with a shiver of revulsion.

"And," Jessie prompted.

"And computers," Screech said. "It's not only a requirement for graduation, it's a requirement for getting into college."

"Ew," Lisa murmured. "That's right. And we are all planning to go to college somewhere next year."

"Exactly," Jessie said. "I know that Screech has his computer credits covered, and so do I. What about the rest of you?"

"Er, not exactly," Zack confessed.

"Me neither," Kelly said.

"Or me," Slater groaned.

"Ew," Lisa moaned. "I put off getting my computer credit until this year, too. What can we do?"

"Not graduate?" Zack offered weakly.

Lisa shook her head determinedly. "That is not an option. I don't think the college admissions boards will take this disaster into consideration when they look at our records. You think maybe they'll just give us the credit because we signed up for the class?"

"Not likely," Jessie said. "Perhaps you'll be able to use the computer lab at another school at night."

"Night school?" Kelly gasped. "But what about those of us who have jobs after school? If I don't work now to save for it, I won't be able to even go on to college!"

Slater slumped lower in his seat. "If only computers weren't so important these days."

"Oh, I wouldn't say they were important," Screech said, twisting in his chair to look back at Zack, Kelly, and Slater.

"They aren't?" Kelly asked, her blue eyes wide with hope.

"No, it's more like they are necessary," Screech explained.

"Necessary." Zack heaved a giant sigh. "You know, Screech, that doesn't make me feel any better."

"I wish I knew who decided to start using computers," Lisa grumbled.

"Well, I think his name was Smith," Screech told her, "but why do you want to know?"

"So I can kick him," she said.

"You're kidding about the guy's name, right?" Zack insisted. "Smith?"

"No," Screech said, his expression a bit distant as he considered the matter. "It was Smith, all right."

"He was the head of an airline," Jessie added.

"Trust you to know," Slater murmured under his breath.

"As I understand it, he met another man also named Smith during a long flight. Well, this Smith worked for a computer technology firm that had just invented a giant networking system for the military. From the things he told the airline Smith that the computer could do, they devised a plan to use a similar system to make plane reservations more efficient. When it was a big success, other businesses jumped on the bandwagon and, poof, the computer age was born," Jessie explained.

"And a big headache was created for high school students," Lisa said.

Kelly rubbed her forehead. "I think I'm getting one now just worrying about graduating."

Slater took her hand in his and patted it, ignoring the way Zack glared at him. "Don't fret. I'm sure Belding has a plan."

As if he'd heard them, up on the stage Mr. Belding got a harried expression on his face. "I'm very glad you asked that question," he told his audience. "Yes, we all realize that some of our seniors need computer credits to graduate. Unfortunately, all the computer labs at the other high schools are used after regular school hours for honors projects and community education programs. The only option we can offer, therefore, is for those seniors concerned to take the summer course in computers at Valley High or return to Bayside in the fall when our lab is back in working order. In either case, these students would be forced to delay graduation until the end of summer or next winter."

The gang all exchanged wide-eyed, and slightly frantic, looks.

"We're doomed!" Lisa groaned.

"We're dead," Slater said.

"Good-bye college," Kelly sighed.

"Farewell glowing future," Zack said.

"They can't do that to you!" Jessie exclaimed.

"Just watch them," Slater told her.

"There's got to be something we can do." Jessie grabbed Screech's arm and shook it. "Think! You know more about computers than anyone else, Screech. There has got to be a solution that's better than this."

Obediently, he wrinkled his forehead in thought, but it looked like a painful process. "I could volunteer to help repair the terminals," he said at length.

"Great! I'll bet some of the other nerds are good at fixing PCs, too. Do you think they'd volunteer their time for the good of the school?" Jessie asked.

"They sure would!" Screech announced, brightening at the thought. A moment later, though, his mobile face fell. "But it won't be enough. Even with all of us working, there are still supplies to buy and our own classes to take. The school year would be nearly over by the time the lab was working again."

"You're kidding!" Jessie insisted.

"You heard the full extent of the damage," he said.

"Then there's just one thing to do," Zack said. Since Slater was still holding Kelly's hand, Zack took her other one in his and squeezed it gently.

She looked up at him, her expression sad. "That's right," she agreed. "There is only one thing to do."

Lisa frowned at them. "What are you talking about?"

Reluctantly, Slater released Kelly's hand. "What else?" he said. "Preppie's got to scam us a solution."

"And he's got to do it fast," Kelly added. "Really fast."

Chapter 3

▲　▼　▲　▼　▲

Jessie scowled at her friends. "Scamming is not the solution."

"But I'm so good at it," Zack insisted.

"He is, you know," Lisa said.

"I just think we need to be more adult about this. There must be legal processes we can follow," Jessie said.

"So speaks our future lawyer," Slater murmured. "Sure those hours you spend hanging out at your future stepfather's law office haven't warped what used to pass for good sense?"

Not long before, Jessie's mother had surprised everyone by accepting a marriage proposal from Kenyon Sinclair, a successful Palisades lawyer. Jessie had then stunned her friends by being pleased about her mother's forthcoming marriage. She hadn't been happy about her mom's previous boyfriends, so the fact that she adored Kenyon made everyone happy.

Except her friends when she talked on and on about life in a legal office.

"Do you have another solution?" Lisa asked. "Because if you don't, I'm voting for a scammeister special."

"Me, too," Slater said. "After all, we don't need the computer lab operational to prove we're computer literate. We just have to demonstrate our ability."

Jessie folded her arms across her chest. "As much as you'd like it to count, I'm afraid that scoring monster points on Mutant Alien Space Buddies is not the same as being able to program a computer."

"Well, it should be," Zack said. Mutant Alien Space Buddies was the most popular video game at Bayside, and he'd spent hours at the Max pumping quarters into the machine to save the universe from invasion, not to mention to insure that his name appeared at the top of the list of master players.

Jessie tapped one finger against her cheek as she thought. "We need more data."

"Data? If you ask me, Jess has been spending too much time at a computer keyboard already," Lisa whispered to Kelly, pulling her aside so that Jessie wouldn't overhear them.

"Well, she hasn't been on a date with anyone she really cares about in a long time," Kelly whispered back. "I've been hoping she'd meet someone at Mr. Sinclair's office and fall in love. It can't be easy for her. I mean, everybody around her is in love. You've got Keith . . ."

Lisa sighed happily. She'd been going with Keith Bockman, a dreamy hunk on the Bayside tennis team, for weeks now. Life was perfect. Or it was when the tennis team wasn't traveling to play against another school and he was gone. It was great to have a jock worship the ground upon which a girl walked, but if he wasn't around enough to be seen doing it, some of the enjoyment was lacking.

". . . and I've got Zack," Kelly continued. "With her mom planning her wedding, Jessie can't help but feel a little left out without a sweetheart of her own."

"True," Lisa admitted. "Maybe we should try to find her one. She sure won't stumble over a hunk while she's crusading for the computer lab. Great-looking guys aren't exactly plentiful in geekland."

"Sad but true," Kelly agreed.

"What are you two whispering about?" Jessie asked. "If you've got an idea, share it with us."

Kelly and Lisa exchanged a leery look.

"Golly, I wish we could help," Kelly said. "But the truth is, we weren't talking about the computer lab."

"Nope," Lisa declared. "We were discussing something else entirely."

"Like what?" Slater asked.

Kelly and Lisa looked at each other again.

"Like what?" Kelly echoed.

"Oh, like what!" Lisa cried. "Trust me, it wasn't anything anyone else would be interested in."

"Maybe we would," Jessie said.

"Maybe they would," Kelly hissed at Lisa.

"No, you wouldn't," Lisa insisted. "Because it was . . . it was . . ." She waved her hand in the air while her mind whirled, searching for a convenient lie.

Kelly grabbed Lisa's hand. "We were talking about Lisa's nail polish. Remember how she hated the shade she was wearing yesterday morning? Well, this one is so much better, don't you agree?"

Since only Screech leaned forward to inspect Lisa's long, blushing-peach nails, the subject quickly turned back to ways to resurrect the computer lab. Before any solution was discovered, though, the bell rang to signal the start of the next period, and the gang hurried off to different classrooms.

▲　▼　▲

Jessie picked a business letter from the wire basket and glanced at it quickly, determining which file it belonged in. "So, you see," she explained to the paralegal with whom she was working in

Kenyon's office, "it is really important to think of some spectacular but fast way to raise money. Ready cash seems to be the thing that is keeping the lab from being operational."

"Are you sure?" Edward Sennett asked, adjusting his glasses before sorting through more paperwork. "Perhaps that's only part of the problem. It sounds like human resources are also lacking. Even with your friend and his buddies volunteering their time and expertise, it comes down to the fact that only two people are rebuilding the system full-time."

"Hmm. That's right. We've got twenty-five PCs to repair and a few to replace," Jessie mused.

"All of which is not cheap," Edward reminded her.

"Nothing is cheap," Jessie said with a groan. "In the last few days I've checked into renting computers as well."

"Good idea," Edward said.

"So I thought until I found out how much it would cost to lease two dozen computer terminals for the rest of the school year," Jessie admitted.

"Exactly how much would it run?" Edward asked. When Jessie told him, he flinched. "Ouch! I agree. It would take a sorcerer to come up with that much in a hurry."

Jessie turned away from the filing cabinet to agree and found that a colorful batch of silk flowers had materialized between her and Edward.

"You called for a sorcerer?" a really cute-looking guy asked. He was wearing a suit but had pulled his tie loose and unbuttoned the top button of his shirt. His hair was a soft brown and spilled attractively over his forehead toward eyes that were nearly as blue as those of movie heartthrob Mitch Tobias.

Edward chuckled. "I should have known you'd recognize a cue like that one. I didn't know you'd finished with your interview. What happened? Kenyon toss you out on your ear?"

"Your esteemed Mr. Sinclair has better taste than that," the stranger said, tossing the bouquet aside onto the desk. "He hired me on the spot."

"Great!" Edward cried. "In that case, you'd better meet Jessie Spano, Kenyon's stepdaughter-to-be and future lawyer-in-training. Jessie, meet my best friend, Duncan Connor."

"A pleasure," Jessie said, holding out her hand to the handsome newcomer.

"Indeed it is," Duncan agreed, shaking her hand and then continuing to hold it. "And it's all mine. Do you work for Sinclair, then?"

Jessie smiled and drew her fingers from his grasp. "Not actually. I volunteer because I want to be a lawyer someday."

"Smart woman," Duncan said to Edward. "Which makes me wonder why she's hanging around with you. Does she know all your darkest secrets?"

Edward looked pained. "No, but I suppose you are planning to tell her?"

"Only about this one," Duncan insisted, and reached behind his friend's ear. "I've told you time and time again to wash behind your ears," he said, and dropped a couple of coins into Edward's hand.

Jessie giggled delightedly. "You're a magician!"

Duncan placed a hand over his heart and bowed deeply. "When I'm not a lowly prelaw student," he confessed. "Or a lowly gofer in this magnificent establishment."

"Magnificent?" Jessie asked. She glanced at the white walls, the bank of tall file cabinets, and the long folding table in the center of the room. This was the workroom of Kenyon's firm, the place where research was done and files were stored. The plush atmosphere appeared only in the reception area and in the lawyers' offices.

"Certainly it's magnificent," Duncan said. "Take a deep breath and tell me what you smell."

"Dust?" Jessie suggested.

Duncan inhaled deeply, his eyes closed. "Absolutely not. It's the euphoric aroma of justice."

"Personally," Edward said, "I'm with Jessie. I smell dust."

Duncan perched on a corner of the table. "Okay, so do I, but it's legal-eagle dust. And that's something

I've wanted to have in my lungs for a long time."

"You have not," Edward drawled. "You wanted to be a sorcerer and had to settle for being a magician. I've been watching you practice sleight-of-hand tricks since we were eleven."

"Okay, I lied. My fascination with the law dates from the day I realized that I couldn't make a living out of an ability to levitate roses," Duncan confessed. "But even that's been a good number of years. What about you, Jessie? What draws you to the legal profession?"

Jessie turned back to her filing. "My mother, actually," she told him. "She's a public defender here in Palisades."

Duncan's eyebrows rose out of sight beneath his tousled hair. "Impressive," he murmured. "Does she take after her daughter and have brains as well as beauty?"

Jessie kept her back to him so that he wouldn't see she was blushing. "Well, she has won an impressive number of cases," she admitted, "but she's far more gorgeous than I am."

"Impossible," Duncan said.

Jessie blushed even more.

"So, when do you start work?" Edward asked.

"Two weeks, so I'm still kicking my heels for a while," Duncan said. "You wouldn't happen to know of a kid's birthday party or a carnival in need of someone to pull rabbits out of a hat?"

"Sorry, pal," Edward said. "Wish I could help, but—"

Jessie turned back to them quickly. "What did you say?" she asked.

Edward and Duncan glanced at each other. Duncan shrugged his shoulders, indicating he was feeling as lost as his friend was.

"That I couldn't help Dunc?" Edward offered.

"No, before that. About a carnival."

"That I have rabbits living in my hat?" Duncan suggested. "Not terribly smart or hygienic, I'm sure, but—"

"That's it!" Jessie crowed. "A carnival! Why didn't I think of it before?"

Duncan shook his head. "I haven't the slightest idea."

"But it's so perfect! And it was so successful when we were trying to save Smuggler's Cove," Jessie said, her eyes focused on some inner vision that neither Edward nor Duncan could see.

The young men stared at her, slightly bemused by her enthusiasm.

Jessie came back to earth with a thud. "Oh, I'm sorry. You don't know about that, do you? It happened right when I met Kenyon and started coming to the office."

Edward stacked the papers on the table before him. "Ah yes. I remember. The big man got involved in helping Jessie and her friends while he was evaluating her for a scholarship," he explained to Duncan.

"Did you win it?" the handsome magician asked Jessie.

"Oh yes," she said. "But the really important thing is that we managed to come up with enough money to keep the beach from being sold by the city."

"Ah, an environmentalist, too," Duncan mused. "Smuggler's Cove, hmm? Isn't that an incredibly romantic place?"

"And isolated," Edward added.

Duncan slid off the desk. "Listen, I've got two weeks before I start working for Sinclair, Jessie. How would you like to help a poor undeserving magician kill some of that time? Maybe take in dinner, a movie. A moonlit stroll along the beach at Smuggler's Cove?"

Jessie cocked her head to the side and stared at him. "Do you really have a rabbit in your hat?" she asked.

Duncan grinned. "Actually? No."

"Oh," Jessie said, and sighed.

"It's more like six," Duncan said. "I started with two, but you know how rabbits are. They're such whizzes at math, particularly multiplication. If I show them to you, will you go out with me?"

Jessie smiled. "Honestly? I'd go out with you even if you were rabbitless, but since you do have them . . ." She got a distant look in her eyes again.

"Uh-oh, pal," Edward murmured. "I think you're in big trouble."

Duncan let his gaze rest softly on Jessie's thoughtful face. "Maybe," he said, "but you know what, Ed? I don't mind in the least."

Chapter 4

▲ ▼ ▲ ▼ ▲

Kelly skipped out of her house, half running to meet Zack as he drove up the Kapowski driveway. Before he could park and get out of the car, she had yanked open the passenger door and hopped inside. "Step on it," she urged him. "Jessie says it's important."

"Isn't everything to her?" Zack asked. "Do you know how many times she has claimed it was a life-or-death situation when all she wanted was bodies for a Green Teens demonstration?" Green Teens was the environment group that Jessie belonged to.

"Lots," Kelly said, "but if you were a bird facing extinction, you'd think it was a life-or-death situation. Besides, I know exactly why you're in a snit."

"A what?"

"You're just in a bad mood because she vetoed scamming as a solution to the computer-lab problem," Kelly insisted. "Now, stop sulking, and let's get on our way to Screech's."

"I am not sulking," Zack said, but he did back his car out into the street. "Why are we going to Screech's for this meeting?"

Kelly snapped her seat belt closed. "Because he's our resident computer expert. And he's got some stuff Jessie thinks we should all see. Now stop talking and drive."

Zack did so for thirty seconds. "You know," he mused, gazing at the sky, "it's a real pretty night tonight."

Kelly glanced at the sparkling array of stars above. "Uh-huh," she agreed.

"If Jessie's meeting gets over early, maybe we could take a drive," Zack suggested.

"The only reason Jessie's meeting would be short is if everybody agrees with whatever she suggests," Kelly said.

"I could do that," Zack said. "How about you?"

"Well, yes, I could be agreeable, but I do still have homework to do," Kelly explained, "so I don't think it's a very good idea to tool around tonight."

Zack stared down the street. Ever since Kelly had agreed to go steady with him, it had become harder and harder to conduct this romance. She always seemed to be thinking of something entirely different than he was. Like now, when the scent of the sea in the air and the glow of the moonlight made him want to pull over to the side of the road and kiss her.

"You know, if you turn here and catch High Street, we can trim two minutes off our time and get to the Powers' house faster," Kelly pointed out, motioning for him to zig from his route at the next light.

Yep, they were definitely on different wavelengths, Zack decided.

The light turned red just as he reached it. Zack let the Mustang coast to a stop. "I have a suggestion," he said. "How about if I head west instead, and we skip the meeting. Since we already agreed to agree with whatever Jessie has in mind, we don't even need to be there."

Kelly frowned at him. "But I want to be there," she insisted. "Why wouldn't I? Getting the computer lab up and running is important to me. I want to graduate on time, and so do you."

Well, that was true, Zack admitted. He sighed. "I just wish we could spend some quality time together, Kel," he said.

"Oh, Zack," she murmured softly. "Have I been neglecting you? I don't mean to. How about if I make it up to you on Friday? I'm not working, and there's a double feature at the Sav-a-Buck Cinema."

The light changed and, his mind skipping ahead to Friday night, Zack pulled on through the intersection without taking her suggested turn. "Let me guess," he said. "They're playing back-to-back Mitch Tobias movies."

Ever since Kelly had made friends with the handsome actor during the class trip to New York, Zack had been jealous of Mitch. Now that the guy was a famous movie star who had girls sighing over him left and right, Zack didn't like Mitch any better. Less, in fact.

"No," Kelly said. "Both features are Jean-Pierre Bonjour movies."

Zack nearly braked in surprise. Instead he pulled off to the side of the road. "Bonjour flicks? But you hate martial arts movies."

"Not if I close my eyes at certain spots," Kelly confessed.

Since he closed his eyes a lot whenever she dragged him to a romantic movie, Zack figured he could forgive her that.

"Besides, Jean-Pierre is kind of cute. I don't mind that much. And you've been so nice about taking me to see Mitch's movies, I think it's only fair that we go see what you like. Afterward, maybe we could go back out to Lovers' Lane. The view of the ocean is so pretty from there."

Zack flicked his seat belt open and leaned

across to cup her face between his hands. "I love you, Kelly Kapowski," he whispered before he kissed her.

Kelly smiled happily. "That's good," she told him, "because I love you, too, Zack."

▲　▼　▲

Jessie glanced at her watch. "What's keeping them?" she demanded. She paced to the window and back to where Screech sat at his computer terminal playing a quick game of Mutant Alien Space Buddies with Slater.

"This is great," Slater declared. "I didn't even know this game was available for a home system."

"It isn't," Screech said, yanking hard on his control stick to send his player diving for safety from a laser blast. "This is a variation called Mutant Buddies from Alien Space. I wrote the program for my VR headset."

"Virtual Reality? Whoa!" Slater murmured.

"Watch out!" Lisa yelled. She was perched on a stool between the boys, avidly following the activity on the monitor.

Slater jerked his game stick and made his player roll to the side and aim his blaster at the alien who buzzed past, and gained two hundred points by vaporizing him. "Thanks, Lise. He nearly got me."

"Then I should have kept quiet," she grumbled. "At this rate, I'll never get a chance to play."

Jessie cleared her voice. "If you will all remember, I asked you to meet me here for a reason."

"Which was to see the cool video games," Slater said. He nudged Screech's arm. "How come you never told me about these before? All you ever mentioned was the robot and remote-control lawn mower."

Screech sent his player dodging disaster down a narrow alley and picked up a quick five hundred points in the process. "Well, after the mower hacked up Mr. Belding's prize-winning petunias and the robot cut his cabana to ribbons, I decided to concentrate on games."

"Probably less destructive," Slater agreed, watching with pleasure as his player instigated an impressive explosion on the computer screen. "I'd love to play this as a VR version."

"VR, VR, VR," Lisa grumbled. "That's all I hear anymore. There are even TV shows that have it, but I still don't know what Virtual Reality means."

"You're kidding!" Slater gasped. "It is the coolest thing, Lise."

Jessie coughed a little louder. She tapped her foot. "Excuse me, people, but I believe we have more important things to do than—"

Screech pressed a couple buttons on the keyboard and pushed his game stick away. "Would you like to try VR, Lisa?" he asked.

"Sure!" she exclaimed, then looked toward the

monitor. The game was still in progress, and Slater was playing hard. "What about your game? Won't you lose?"

A slow, sly smile curved Screech's lips. "I put it on auto play. The computer will keep playing at my skill level, so Slater's competition will stay constant."

"Whoa," Slater murmured, his eyes glued to the action on the screen. "That's truly awesome."

Screech shrugged. "Oh, it's nothing," he said modestly. He picked up something that looked like a giant View-Master and smiled at it proudly. "Now this," he insisted softly, "this is really something."

"That's nice," Jessie said, "but if we could wait until Kelly and Zack arrive to have a demonstration."

"I don't want to wait," Lisa whined. "Show me now, Screech. Is this the mysterious VR?"

"Part of it," he said, handing the visorlike thing to her before picking up a strange-looking glove.

Lisa eyed the equipment dubiously. "Not exactly what I'd choose for fashion accessories," she commented.

"Are you kidding?" Jessie asked. "They match Screech's outfit exactly."

"Gosh! You're right!" Lisa gasped as she compared the silver-studded purple glove to Screech's shirt. "Do you make this in any other color?"

"Not yet, but I could for you, my sweet," he told

her. "Would you prefer to do straight VR, or are you daring enough to experience cyberspace?"

Lisa blinked at him in confusion. "Hey, I'm iffy on Virtual Reality without adding cyberspace. What is it anyway?"

"Yeah," Jessie said. "What is cyberspace exactly?"

Screech took another visor down from a shelf and handed it to Jessie. "Find out for yourself," he offered. "VR is a computer-enhanced adventure, but cyberspace is computer-enhanced interaction between two players. By sharing a program, you and Lisa could see if this is what you had in mind, Jessie."

Jessie took one last glance at her watch and held her hand out. "I'm game."

He helped both girls don the special gloves and adjusted the visors over their eyes. Wires trailing from their fingertips, Lisa and Jessie faced each other in opposite chairs.

"Ready?" Screech asked.

"You're sure we won't get electrocuted or anything?" Lisa demanded, no longer positive she wanted to have either a VR or cyberspace experience.

"Trust me," Screech said.

"You sound like Zack does just before something goes wrong with one of his scams," Lisa moaned. Then she gasped. "Wow!"

"Double wow," Jessie breathed.

It didn't look like reality exactly. At least not like things did in the television shows, Lisa thought, but she certainly didn't have the same sensation she'd had while watching Screech and Slater play the game on the computer screen. She felt more like she was inside this program.

There was a computer-generated sky with clouds and a flock of birds flying by. She seemed to be flying, too, but not in a plane. Arms spread, she sailed about, gliding on air currents. Beside her another figure floated as well.

"Is that you, Lisa?" Jessie asked.

"Yes. Is that you?" Lisa asked. "This is really cool!" She tilted her head to look over at Jessie and sent herself into a tailspin, spiraling down to where a river twisted through a green countryside. "Eek! What do I do now?"

"Look up," Jessie urged.

Lisa did so. The ground disappeared as the sky flashed by. Her Virtual Reality character turned in a slow somersault. "Whoa!" she murmured when she finally steadied. "I'm dizzy."

"I've read that VR does that to some people," Jessie said.

"Maybe we need an instruction booklet to read before we try much more of this," Lisa suggested.

"Want to stop, then?" Jessie asked.

"No, I think I'm getting the hang of it. Do you see those birds anywhere?"

As Lisa watched, Jessie's VR figure turned to look around their altered universe. "Over there," she said, gesturing.

"Let's follow them," Lisa suggested.

"How?"

"Hmm. Good question. How do those comic book heroes do it? Or maybe it's like swimming." She stretched one arm out and moved her feet back and forth. "Hey! I'm moving!"

There was a quick rapping at the door, but neither Jessie nor Lisa paid any attention to it. They both had their arms outstretched and were leaning forward in their chairs.

Zack pushed open the door and he and Kelly slid inside the room, their hands linked. Screech and Slater were too busy with their own game to notice their arrival or the soft glow in Kelly's eyes or the contented curve of Zack's mouth.

"Sorry we're late," Zack said. He glanced at the cyberspacing girls and the battling boys. No one bothered to greet them or even comment on the time. "Did we miss much?" he asked.

"Aaagh!" Slater groaned as he wrestled with his control. "That was a close one!"

"Oooh!" Lisa cooed. "Watch this!"

"That's nothing," Jessie said. "Try this."

"Ha-ha-ha-ha!" Screech cackled gleefully. "Take that, sucker!"

Zack and Kelly glanced from one group of their friends to the other and back again.

"You know," Zack finally whispered aside to her, "I don't think anybody even missed us."

Chapter 5

▲　▼　▲　▼　▲

It was a good half hour before everyone was ready to talk about Jessie's carnival idea. Once their friends noticed they had arrived, Zack insisted on challenging Slater to another round of Mutant Buddies from Alien Space while Kelly entered cyberspace. Getting down to business was rather boring and anticlimactic after game playing, though.

"I don't know why we didn't think of this before," Jessie told her friends. "Having a Family Fun Day at Bayside would raise the money we need to boot the computer lab back into working order this year. Proceeds would not only go to buy repair parts and replacement computers, but to hiring technicians to help Mr. Monza and Mr. Hayes."

"You really think we'd make that much money?" Kelly asked. "I mean, none of this stuff is cheap. If it was, the school budget would cover things."

"Well, I thought of that, too," Jessie said. "And when Lisa mentioned she would be studying insurance next week, I stopped by to ask Mr. Belding if the lab equipment was covered by an insurance policy."

"Was it?" Slater asked.

"Yes, but since the terminals and software were old, depreciation on the equipment seriously reduced the amount the insurance company was willing to pay."

Lisa scrambled for her purse and made a note in the small notebook she carried in it. "I've got to remember that," she said. "It ought to help me get an A in the insurance module. And believe me, I can use all the help I can get in the Life Is a Science class. Do you realize they have yet to cover something really important, like how to choose just the right accessories or get the best bargain on a prom dress?"

"It boggles the mind," Zack agreed.

"Won't putting on a carnival be difficult?" Kelly asked. "Especially since we weren't exactly involved in the organization of booths with Save the Beach. It was all your Green Teens friends who handled that while we concentrated on playing volleyball."

"Which we could do again," Jessie said.

"Play a bunch of surfer dudes in a game where we have to win?" Slater murmured. "No thank you."

"Okay, but there are plenty of other things we can do," Jessie insisted.

"Like what?" Lisa asked.

"Like offer visitors the chance to enjoy VR rides as we did a little while ago," Jessie said. She turned to Screech. "How many visors do you have?"

He screwed up his face and thought, ticking off inventory on his fingers. "Personally? Two, but I'm sure I can borrow another eight from members of the computer club."

Jessie beamed at him. "That's ten."

Slater shook his head. "But exactly how exciting is this VR program you girls played? All I heard was *oohs* and *aahs*. When I'm on a carnival ride, I want to get scared and dizzy."

"You take a dive toward the ground as I did, buddy, and your hair will turn white," Lisa advised him.

"One thrill and it's over," Slater insisted. "If I'm paying, I want more than one heart-stopping moment."

"Yeah, like on the Kamikaze Triple Loop at Palisades amusement park," Zack said.

"Whoa, yes!" Slater agreed enthusiastically. "You can't get a thrill like that with VR."

"You can with cyberspace," Screech said.

"You can?" Zack and Slater asked in unison.

"Sure, it's easy. All it takes is for one person to control the program and another to experience it," Screech explained. "Cathy Lynn Carmody has been working on a roller-coaster program that we could use."

"Yes!" Zack and Slater shouted.

Jessie scribbled on her clipboard. "It looks like we have at least one ride, but not everyone is into VR, or wants to be."

"And since we want families to come to the carnival, we need a lot of things for younger children, too," Kelly said. "I know my little brother Billy wouldn't be interested in VR, but he'd love to have a ride on a pony."

"Who wouldn't!" Screech cried happily.

Lisa scooted a little farther away from him. "Where are we going to find ponies, though?"

"I suppose we could rent them," Jessie said, "but I'd really like to not spend much in putting this together. I mean, the object is to make money."

"How about if I ask my uncle Dan to donate the use of the ponies?" Kelly suggested. "He doesn't live very far outside of Palisades and he's got lots of ponies. I'd even volunteer to supervise the rides."

Jessie grinned widely. "Perfect!" she breathed. "Now what other suggestions can we come up with? It would be really great to be able to explain in more detail what we are planning to do so we can get Mr. Belding's and the school board's permission."

Zack stretched out his legs and got comfortable in a beanbag chair. "Oh, that part is easy," he drawled, tilting his head back and closing his eyes. "All you have to do is pitch the idea right."

"Exactly," Jessie said. "Which is why I think we should choose the pitch person carefully. This person would have to understand what we are planning to do."

"The person would have to want it to be successful," Kelly added.

"Would have to have a history of getting people to agree to do things," Lisa said.

"Especially when they don't want to do them," Screech contributed.

"And the individual would have to benefit personally from the carnival, being rewarded with something important, oh, say, like being able to graduate in June," Slater said.

"All sounds good to me," Zack murmured sleepily. "Who'd you have in mind?"

When no one answered, he opened his eyes. His friends were all grinning at him.

▲   ▼   ▲

"And so you see, sir, we've got things pretty much covered," Zack told Mr. Belding the next morning. "All we need is the okay and a call for volunteers."

The principal leaned forward in his chair. "I think it's a great idea," he said. "And with so many seniors in need of computer credits, I don't think finding carnival workers will be a problem. When would you like to have this carnival?"

Zack assumed his most concerned expression. "I'm sure you'll agree that the situation is a serious one, Mr. B., so the sooner we can get the lab back in operation, the better. It may sound like short notice, but we're confident that we can pull this together by this weekend."

"That's pretty fast planning," the principal noted.

"It has to be," Zack said. Of course, he wouldn't be the one doing most of the work. He'd thought of some involved excuses to use in the event Jessie cornered him when she went looking for help.

"I'm especially impressed that the computer club is handling most of the rides," Mr. Belding said. "But, since the computer lab benefits from this, the idea of using Virtual Reality as rides is great. And the ponies are a nice touch. Now, what other ideas have you and the gang come up with?"

Zack fished in his pocket for the list Jessie had given him. "Lisa is calling her godfather, who is in administration at Palisades General, and seeing if we can borrow the dunking machine the hospital uses at their fund-raising fairs."

"You wouldn't be volunteering to be one of the people getting dunked, would you, Zack?" Mr. Belding asked hopefully.

Zack ignored the question. "Then Slater is planning on having members of the wrestling and football teams challenge carnival-goers to arm wrestle."

"I'd like to take them on myself," the principal admitted. "I was quite the athlete in college, you know."

Rather than let Mr. Belding spin out what he was sure would be a boring memory, Zack forged ahead. "I was thinking of running a dart toss if I can get local businesses to donate prizes."

"Can't think of anyone more likely to be successful doing that than you, Zack," Mr. Belding declared with a chuckle.

"And Jessie knows a magician who is willing to be part of the midway entertainments," Zack concluded.

"A magician! Now there's a profession I once thought of pursuing. Of course, that was before I met Mrs. Belding and she put a stop to the idea. I can still do some pretty fancy card tricks, though. In fact, I think I've got a deck here in my desk."

Zack pushed out of his chair, intent on escaping. "I'd like to see them sometime, sir," he insisted hardily, if insincerely. "But right now, don't you think we should get the school board's approval for the carnival?"

Mr. Belding snapped his fingers and winked. "Absolutely right, Zack. I'll call them immediately."

When Zack left the principal's office a few

minutes later, he barely got the door shut before he collapsed back against it.

"Well?" Jessie demanded, rushing anxiously to his side. "Do we go ahead with everything?"

"Yep," Zack said. "In fact, the whole school board promised to attend."

"Oh, Zack! That's great!" She threw her arms around his neck and hugged him. "Gosh! There is so much to be done! What should I do first? Talk to Ms. Meadows about snacks maybe?"

"Mmm, cotton candy, caramel apples, and waffle cones with ice cream," Zack murmured dreamily.

"Certainly not," Jessie declared. "Frozen rice cream dipped in carob possibly, but nothing with sugar in it." Before Zack could protest, she dashed off.

▲　▼　▲

The first posters advertising the Recompute Bayside carnival were up by lunch period. Jessie and Kelly sat at a table in the hall outside the cafeteria, surrounded by students eager to volunteer. Screech had another sign-up area outside the computer lab, and Lisa and Slater were in charge of one by the gymnasium. Zack spent his time convincing various teachers to volunteer for the dunking booth. By the end of the school day another dozen entertainment booths had been born, planned, and fully staffed, and Zack was hoarse from talking.

When the last bell sounded, the gang dragged outside, exhausted with all they'd done. "And we would have accomplished even more if we hadn't had to attend classes," Lisa complained.

The guys melted away quickly, escaping before Jessie could suggest another meeting or sign them up for another committee.

But Jessie was as wilted as her friends, her feet dragging more with each step she took. When a brightly colored bunch of phony flowers materialized under her nose, she forgot all about being tired.

"Duncan!" she cried. "What are you doing here?"

The handsome magician handed over the bouquet. "Just checking on my lovely assistant. And if we're still on for dinner tonight. You did promise to show me Smuggler's Cove in the moonlight, remember?"

"I remember," Jessie said shyly.

Lisa was coming down the school steps behind Kelly, but when she caught sight of Jessie and Duncan and overheard the words *Smuggler's Cove*, she grabbed Kelly's shoulder.

"Hey!" Kelly complained. "You're digging your nails into me."

"Who is that gorgeous hunk?" Lisa demanded faintly.

"Where?" Kelly asked.

Lisa's nails bit deeper. "With Jessie," she hissed.

"With . . . ? Oh, gosh!" Kelly gasped. "Doesn't he look just like that cute guy in—"

"Yes," Lisa said, not letting Kelly finish. "Exactly like him. He's even better looking than—"

"Boy, is he ever," Kelly agreed.

While they watched, the handsome young man took a handkerchief from his pocket, tied a knot in the center, stuffed it slowly and carefully into his fist, and pulled it out again. Only the knot was now missing.

Lisa and Kelly looked at each other. "The magician!" they breathed in unison, and dashed over to where Jessie and her new friend stood.

"Hi," Lisa said, edging next to Duncan. "I'm Lisa Turtle, Jessie's best friend."

Kelly pushed closer. "And I'm Kelly Kapowski, Jessie's other best friend."

Duncan made a motion in the air with his hand and plucked a business card from nothingness. He did the maneuver again, then handed one to each of the girls.

"Connor the Conjurer, at your service. But you can call me Duncan," he told them.

"We're so thrilled you'll be helping us at the carnival," Kelly said.

"We had no idea that Jessie knew someone like you at all," Lisa added, tossing Jessie a hurt look. "She never mentioned you until last night."

"And she didn't tell us much," Kelly said.

"Yeah, like how handsome you are," Lisa said.

Duncan laughed. "Who, me? Naw, I'm just an average guy working my way through school."

Lisa and Kelly exchanged a speaking look.

"I only met Duncan yesterday afternoon after school," Jessie explained.

Duncan grinned at her. "It was the happiest afternoon of my life."

Kelly and Lisa sighed happily.

Jessie clutched the silk flowers to her chest and gazed at Duncan dreamily. "I wasn't expecting to see you until later," she said.

"I know." Duncan leaned closer to her and dropped his voice to a whisper. "But I couldn't stay away any longer. Do you realize that it has been twenty-two hours, seventeen minutes, and"—he glanced at his watch—"forty-two seconds since we parted?"

"Funny," Jessie said. "It seems longer somehow."

Duncan chuckled and offered her his arm. "How about ending my misery this minute by running away with me?"

Jessie slid her hand into the crook of his arm and twinkled up at him. "I thought you'd never ask," she declared.

Chapter 6

▲ ▼ ▲ ▼ ▲

Lisa and Kelly stared after their friend.

"Who was that?" Lisa asked.

Kelly glanced down at the business card she still clutched in her hand. "Duncan Connor."

"That's not what I mean. Think about it. That was not our Jessie," Lisa insisted. "Our Jessie does not forget all about her pet projects and waltz off with a guy."

"Ah, but what a guy," Kelly murmured softly. "I'd sure forget everything but him."

"Me, too," Lisa admitted, "but that's us, not Jessie."

"She's in love," Kelly said. "Just like we wanted her to be."

"But not right now," Lisa hissed. "If she isn't available to answer questions and boss everyone around, what will happen to the carnival?"

"Oh," Kelly mumbled with a gulp. "You don't think that the volunteers will pester us instead, do you?"

"You bet they will. They'll figure that we know as much about everything as she does because we're her friends," Lisa said.

"But we don't!" Kelly cried. "Golly! What should we do?"

Lisa thought a moment. "Break up Jessie's romance?"

Kelly shook her head. "No, not that. We were just wishing she could be in love so she wouldn't feel left out of things. And Duncan seems really nice."

"He's sure romantic," Lisa said. "I wish Keith was. Do you think he could take lessons from Duncan?"

"Oh, I don't know," Kelly murmured. "Keith seemed awfully romantic when he brought you those delicious pastries when we were all trying to get you to eat."

"True," Lisa admitted, thinking back to her brief but agonizing bout with anorexia nervosa. "But he's never counted the seconds until he could see me again, or looked at me the way Duncan looked at Jessie."

"Yeah," Kelly sighed deeply. "Zack never does those things, either. Oh, he tells me he loves me, but I already know that. It just isn't the same, you know?"

"Do I ever," Lisa said. She stared off down the street in the direction Duncan's car had disappeared. "Maybe it has something to do with Duncan being older."

"You think?"

"Well, it's worth a shot," Lisa insisted. "I mean, he is a student, and I'd say he's been in college for a couple years, wouldn't you?"

Kelly shrugged. "I don't know. Maybe Duncan's just trying to impress her because of her mom or Kenyon."

Lisa shook her head. "No way. Not with the way he was looking at her. Nope, that was L-O-V-E."

"Do you think he fell in love with her at first sight?" Kelly asked.

"Or Jessie with him? Boy, if I were in her shoes, I sure would," Lisa admitted.

Kelly sighed wistfully again. "Me, too."

▲　▼　▲

Slater barely glanced at the black car as it cruised down the street past him. But a moment later his head whipped around. Jessie had been in the passenger seat, he realized. That couldn't be right, because Jess always drove herself to school.

Had she experienced car trouble? Was the battery dead? A tire flat? What was she doing in a low-slung black sports car?

Well, it had been an older model, and, now that he thought about it, there had been a slight knock in the engine, and the body could have done with a new paint job. But none of that explained why Jessie had been hitching a ride.

"Who was that taking Jessie home?" Zack asked, loping across the parking lot from his own car. "I don't remember ever seeing him before."

Him? Slater frowned and gazed off down the street again.

"Somebody from Kenyon's office, do you think?"

"Could be," Slater admitted. "For the last few weeks, she's been working there after school for a couple hours a day."

"Wonder why she didn't drive herself?" Zack mused.

"Maybe parking is a problem," Slater suggested. "Sinclair's office is downtown."

"Right," Zack said. "Convenient of them to have such a good-looking guy they can send to pick her up."

"Good-looking?" Slater repeated.

"If you like the type," Zack said. "Considering the way Kelly sighed over the guy in that movie with all the weddings, I guess girls do like the type."

"Mmm," Slater mumbled.

"'Course, what do you care who Jessie dates?" Zack continued. "You both decided to break up, right?"

"Right," Slater growled, still staring down the street. Breaking up didn't mean you stopped caring, though.

▲   ▼   ▲

First period was almost over when the intercom in Zack's classroom buzzed.

"Mrs. Thornapple?" a familiar voice asked.

"Yes, Mr. Belding?" the teacher answered as she leaned over her desk and held the speaker button down.

"Would you please send Zack Morris to my office?"

Zack swallowed loudly. Now what had he done? Well, and got caught for doing, that is.

"Certainly, Mr. Belding," Mrs. Thornapple said, straightening. "You heard, Mr. Morris?"

Zack pulled himself up from his desk. "I heard."

The halls were deserted; not even the keen-eyed monitors were in evidence. Zack took his time, strolling along at a casual pace, books under his arm. The bell rang before he reached the school office, so Zack used the mad rush of students heading for new classrooms to delay his arrival even longer. But when he opened the door to Mr. Belding's lair, he made a show of breathing heavily as if he'd hurried.

"You wanted . . . to . . . see . . . me?" he gasped, dropping into the chair before the principal's desk.

"Yes, I did, Morris," Mr. Belding said sternly. "I'm very disappointed in you, Zack. Very disappointed."

Zack tried not to look worried. "You are, sir?"

The principal shook his head sadly from side to

side. "I thought we understood each other, son. I thought we had a bond."

"A bond," Zack repeated.

"We've spent a lot of time together over the last few years," Mr. Belding said. "I can't say I've done the same with any other student."

"Is this good or bad?" Zack asked.

"I'm hurt, Zack. I thought . . . but I guess I was wrong."

"Sir?"

Mr. Belding leaned forward, resting his arms on his desk. "Is it because I'm the principal? Is that why you felt you couldn't ask me?"

Still at a loss, Zack fidgeted in his chair. "Ask you what, sir?"

Mr. Belding looked stunned for a moment. "You mean, you don't know?"

Zack shook his head slowly, not ready to confess to anything, just in case he confessed to the wrong thing.

"The dunk tank," Mr. Belding said.

"The dunk tank! *You* want to volunteer to be dunked?"

"It's for a good cause," the principal insisted.

Zack dug his list of suckers . . . er, volunteers out of his pocket. "I'd be proud to have you be one of our celebrity dunkees, Mr. B."

Mr. Belding beamed happily. "I'm proud to be among them," he said.

Zack consulted his paper. "Two o'clock? You only need to do it for fifteen minutes, then it will be Mr. Hayes's turn."

"Don't tell me you only need me for that one brief time," Mr. Belding said. "There's no need to take it easy on me, Zack. I'm more than willing to pull my weight. So to speak."

The offer was too good to pass up. "Well," Zack drawled lazily, "we were hoping to find someone to take the 9:30 shift that morning, but it's for thirty long minutes."

"I can do that," the principal promised, then paused. "But doesn't the fair open at ten?"

"Oh, sure. This is the early-bird shift. It allows the fair workers to enjoy certain features of the carnival before it officially opens," Zack explained, inventing as he went. "This way they'll be donating cash to the fund as well as their time."

"Say, that's a very good idea," Mr. Belding said. "I'm glad I could help." He rubbed his hands together in a greedy gesture. "There's nothing I like better than emptying people's pockets for a good cause."

Zack grinned. "Me, too, sir. Me, too."

▲   ▼   ▲

Kelly had to push her way through a crowd of students at lunch that day. They stood three deep around the gang's usual table and every one of them seemed to be talking at once. Twice she nearly ended up wearing her food.

"But I need to talk to somebody about this right now," Daisy Tyler whined.

"If I don't let them know within the hour, we'll lose both the fishpond and the poles," Dee Dee Horwitzer insisted.

"Like, do I hafta use my right arm for this arm wrestling stuff?" Mac Zarillo grunted. "It's like my good arm, ya know?"

"If I could just talk to Jessie," Phyllis Ptowski said, "I'm sure she'd agree that fortune-telling is always a part of any carnival."

"The band can't set up that close to the dunk tank, I'm telling you," Greg Tolan shouted. "One good splash and you'll electrocute the guitar players."

"All I'm saying, man, is that I can do it. I'll even leap my bike over six cars if you want," Denny Vane offered.

Kelly finally managed to slide into a spot at the table. Lisa, Screech, and Slater were already there, each trying their best to eat lunch. Every time one of them got a fork even close to her or his mouth, another student interrupted with a new demand.

"I could dance when the band takes a break," Toby Welliver said. "I just want a yes or a no. Jessie would give me an answer. Where is she?"

Kelly was wondering that herself.

"We don't know where she is," Lisa snapped at the insistent students.

"All I want is an answer," Phyllis insisted. "If Jessie can't give me one, then who can?"

"Yeah," someone else shouted. "Who's in charge of this carnival?"

"Well, it's not me," Lisa growled.

"Or me," Kelly hastily added.

Screech's face was tight, his eyeballs bugging out. He swallowed loudly, and his Adam's apple bounced up and down his long neck. "Not me, either," he squeaked.

All eyes centered on Slater. "Now wait a minute. Doesn't it stand to reason that the person in charge has to know thousands of details and, no matter what happens, manage to keep every-body happy?"

"Yeah, so?" Denny Vane asked.

"So I'm not the guy, all right?" Slater snarled.

"Well, who is, then?" Daisy demanded.

Slater got out of his seat and, standing on his chair, looked over the heads of the crowd, scanning the cafeteria for Jessie. Or inspiration. Whichever came first.

A slow smile curved his lips and etched deep dimples in his cheeks when another student strolled into the room.

"There he is," Slater told the rabid volunteers.

"Where?" they demanded, craning their necks.

"Over there. You have a problem, just take it to Zack Morris," Slater said. "Has anyone ever known him *not* to have an answer?"

The crowd surged as one toward Zack, cornering him before he realized they were even after him.

Slater sat back down in his seat and picked up his fork. "You were saying?" he asked Lisa.

She chewed quickly, one eye on the clock. "I can't remember what we were talking about anymore," she confessed. "That horde descended on us so fast, they took me by surprise."

"You were about to tell me what happened to Jessie," he reminded her.

"Oh, that. Duncan picked her up for lunch," Lisa said.

"He did? Oooh, that is so sweet," Kelly crooned.

"Who's Duncan?" Slater demanded.

Lisa shoveled another bite of lunch into her mouth. "The magician," she mumbled. "They're working on an act for the carnival." She grinned. "By the way, that was fast thinking, siccing everybody on Zack."

"I couldn't think of a more deserving person," Slater said.

Kelly giggled. "He does have a habit of worming his way out of work, doesn't he? Well, this will serve him right."

"I'm glad you agree," Slater murmured. "Now, about this Duncan guy."

Lisa wasn't prepared to give out information, though. She turned to Kelly. "What's this I hear about a kissing booth?"

Kelly's eyes brightened. "Great idea, isn't it? The cheerleaders are going to run it," she said. "Just a dollar a kiss and, since we decided to just string a crepe-paper barrier between two trees rather than have a real booth, we have next to no overhead. All the money we take in will go to save the computers."

"You'll make a fortune," Lisa foretold. "It makes me almost sad I resigned from the squad."

"I just have one problem," Kelly confessed. "I've got to be in two places at one time."

"That's a tough one," Slater agreed. "Now, when exactly did Jessie meet this magician dude?"

Nobody paid any attention to his question.

"What are you going to do, Kelly?" Screech asked.

"Well, since I'm head cheerleader, I can't very well not be at the kissing booth, so I've got to find somebody to replace me at the rides," Kelly said.

"At the rides?" Lisa echoed, her mind on the fun she'd had using Screech's VR visor. "Heck, I'll do that for you."

"You will?" Kelly cried. She jumped out of her seat and hugged her friend. "You're absolutely wonderful!"

"Are you kidding? I can't wait," Lisa said.

"I can't, either," Kelly said. "I know you're just going to love the ponies."

Lisa's mouth dropped open. "Ponies?" she whispered weakly.

Chapter 7

▲ ▼ ▲ ▼ ▲

"Wow! Ponies!" Screech shouted. "Can I help, too?"

"Just help?" Lisa asked. "You sure you don't want to be in charge of them, period?"

Screech sighed deeply. "I only wish I could, but I'm in charge of the Virtual Reality rides. Although most of the computer club has been working with VR, no one knows as much about it as I do."

"Just my luck," Lisa mumbled.

Across the room, the mob of students was still shouting questions at Zack.

Kelly stared at the ruckus. "Do you think he can handle things?"

"Zack?" Slater scoffed. "You're kidding me.

This is the guy who has talked his way out of so many scrapes, I've lost count."

"But this is different," Kelly insisted. "We want the carnival to be a success. If Zack doesn't take it seriously, can it be?"

"Zack knows this is important," Screech said. "He won't fail us."

Kelly propped her chin in her hand, her eyes still on the milling students. "I sure hope you're right," she said.

"So do I," Slater said. "Now, let's get back to this Duncan guy. What exactly do you know about him?"

▲　▼　▲

Jessie sipped on her soda and stared across the sand at Duncan. "This is so nice of you," she said. "I can't tell you the last time I was off campus for lunch, much less at the beach for a picnic."

"I'm glad you're enjoying it, although gourmet cuisine this ain't," he quipped, holding up his own peanut butter sandwich. "But when you hang around with a struggling student, I'm afraid this is fairly normal fare."

Jessie took a bite of her sandwich, finding the taste of white bread, peanut butter, and grape jelly rather foreign to her taste buds. She wasn't about to point out to her handsome date that it would be healthier to eat whole-wheat bread and avoid the fat in peanut butter and the sugar in jelly. At least not yet. If he continued to be as fascinated with her as she was with him, she would hint him toward a better diet.

At the moment, though, she simply smiled happily at him. "It's delicious, Duncan, but shouldn't you be at work or school right now?"

"And miss this time with you? Are you kidding, Jessie? You walked into my life at just the right moment. Classes aren't in session, and my job with Sinclair and Associates doesn't start for over a week yet. There isn't a party in search of a magician to perform in all of Palisades, and so I'm totally yours."

He took her hand and kissed the back of it gently. "But then, if I didn't have time to spend with you, I know I'd go nuts. We only just met, but you have already become very special to me."

"And you to me," Jessie assured him. She let her hand linger in his. "I really appreciate your donating your time to the carnival."

Duncan turned to look out to sea. The surf was gentle and the beach was nearly deserted. Only a few tourists, mothers with young children, and retired couples were in sight. "Is that all I mean to you? A convenient entertainer willing to work for free at your fund-raiser?"

"Of course not," Jessie soothed. He was the most wonderful thing to happen to her in a long time, but she didn't think she should tell him. At least not yet. He said a lot of wonderful, wildly romantic things to her, but Jessie was afraid that he had said them to other girls in the past. They were simply what he thought she wanted to hear, so he said them. If he meant them—Jessie sighed dreamily at the idea—she would be in heaven. In love.

She was beginning to think she was already.

Jessie squeezed Duncan's hand. "It's fun learning to be a magician's assistant and learning the secret to how you do all those wonderful tricks, but most of all, I enjoy being with you. I miss you when you aren't around," she confessed.

Duncan stretched out, his head in her lap, her hand still held lightly in his. "Miss me a little or miss me a lot?"

"A lot."

He smiled happily. "If I could stay here with you all day, I'd be a very happy man. It's so peaceful, so beautiful. Not, of course, as gorgeous as Smuggler's Cove. Now there is a place to remember."

Jessie blushed softly, thinking about their visit to the secluded beach. They had shared their first kiss there; the sound of the waves crashing against the rocks created a natural background music she would always cherish. She had walked through the sand at the cove with other dates before, Slater in particular, but those evenings had been nothing like the one she spent with Duncan. It had been special. Magical.

Jessie smoothed Duncan's hair, combing it with

her fingers. "We really should leave," she told him. "I have to get back to school. The lunch period is almost over."

"Pesky thing, reality," he murmured. "While you sit in class, I'll stare at the clock, waiting for the moment you're with me again."

Jessie doubted she'd be able to pay attention in class. She'd have her own eye on the clock, willing the time to fly.

"If you aren't busy this afternoon, can we practice the magic act again?" she asked.

Duncan sat up and got to his feet. He pulled Jessie up after him. "It just so happens that I am busy this afternoon," he said.

When her face fell with disappointment, he took her chin between his thumb and forefinger and tilted her face up. "But I'm busy sharing it with the most beautiful girl I know."

"Me?" Jessie asked hopefully.

He smiled down into her upturned face. "You," he said, and brushed his mouth against hers in a butterfly-brief kiss.

▲   ▼   ▲

Zack was lying in wait for Jessie when she walked into government class.

Or rather floated into it.

Which was very un-Jessie-like. Her step and manner were always purposeful. She was always on a mission.

Except for now, when everyone needed her to be on one.

Zack slid into the empty desk next to the one she took. "Boy, am I glad to see you," he said. "There are a lot of details that need to be decided about the carnival."

"There are?" Jessie asked, her voice dreamy rather than decisive.

Zack had the feeling Jessie's mind was elsewhere. Some place it had never been as long as he had known her. And they'd lived next door to each other since kindergarten.

Sure that once he started listing the questions, suggestions, and problems the students had hurled at him in the cafeteria, Jessie would become her familiar old self, Zack launched into them.

"Phyllis wants to run a fortune telling booth; Greg wants to relocate the stage; Denny wants to play daredevil and jump his bike over a bunch of cars; Toby is willing to dance; and Daisy, Dee Dee, and Mac couldn't wait for you to get back on school grounds before they had their answers," he explained.

Jessie's eyes refocused, but her expression didn't change much, Zack noticed disconcertedly. "Does that mean Daisy, Dee Dee, and Mac's problems were solved?" she asked.

"In a manner of speaking," Zack said. "I told them yes, yes, and no. In that order," he hastened to add, without mentioning what the problems had entailed.

Rather than grill him for details, like the old Jessie would have done, the new one gave him an angelic smile. "Thank you for taking care of things, Zack."

"No sweat," he assured her. "But the rest of them will need answers before the day is finished. You will be around after the final bell today, won't you?"

Jessie didn't answer his question. Instead, she threw out some questions of her own. "What do you think about Phyllis's idea?"

"I think having a fortune-teller would be cool."

"And the stage? Should we move it?"

"Well, considering that the computers got electrocuted in the storm, it's probably a bad idea to do the same to the band if water from the dunk tank splashes on their amplifiers," Zack admitted.

"What about Toby's dancing?"

Zack made a face. "I'd say no if it's going to be that tap dance stuff he does, but if he does cool stuff like break dancing and retro disco, then the answer would be yes."

"And Denny's offer?"

Zack shivered at the thought. "Hey, I like a good motorcycle jump as much as the next guy, but we're talking Bayside here. There will be a lot of little kids running around that day who might decide to try a daredevil act at home and get hurt. And I don't think it would be a good idea to have Denny break every bone in his body just to benefit the computer lab."

"So tell him no," Jessie suggested.

Zack stared at her. "Me!"

"Everything you've said is well thought-out and logical," Jessie said.

"It is?"

She patted him on the shoulder. "You're doing a wonderful job, Zack. I'm so glad I have friends like you to count on."

"But . . . ," he sputtered.

The bell rang, signaling the start of class.

"Thanks, Zack," Jessie said. "Since I've never been a magician's assistant before, Duncan and I really need to practice."

Zack stared at her aghast. "Jessie," he begged.

At the front of the room, Mr. Konopke cleared his throat. "Do you have something to contribute to the class, Morris?" he demanded sternly. "If not, will everyone please turn to page one hundred three in your textbooks."

Zack leafed to the correct section, but the words on the page faded before his eyes. A clipboard with carnival lists surfaced instead. The vision depressed him even more than Mr. Konopke's lecture usually did.

▲   ▼   ▲

Later that day Zack sat crosslegged on the hood of his car, studying the sheets of paper on the clipboard Jessie had given him before skipping off to meet Duncan.

"You know," he mumbled aside to Slater, who leaned against the bumper, his muscular arms folded over his chest, "there are a lot of things missing on these lists of Jessie's."

"You're kidding," Slater insisted. "We're talking Ms. Efficiency here."

"Ms. Former Efficiency, you mean," Zack corrected. "She's acting more like Lisa than like Jessie."

"Yeah," Slater grumbled. "Weird, huh?"

"More than weird," Zack said.

"She never acted like this over me," Slater said.

"Mmm," Zack mumbled, flipping through sheets of paper.

"What's this Duncan dude got that I haven't?" Slater asked.

"Jessie?" Zack suggested.

Slater scowled at him.

"Do you know there is not one mention of a bearded lady in any of Jessie's notes?" Zack demanded.

"Not politically correct, I suppose," Slater said. "I'll bet I could beat the magician at arm wrestling within five seconds."

"Not a chance," Zack said.

"Don't give me that. The guy doesn't have muscles like mine," Slater insisted.

"Doesn't need them," Zack pointed out. "He's

crafty. Has to be to be a magician. All he needs to do is distract you and, bingo, you're pinned and he's a hero."

"I'm not dumb enough to lose my concentration if a guy says 'Will you look at that!'" Slater insisted.

"But you would if he suddenly pulled a quarter from behind your ear," Zack said. "I overheard Jessie telling the girls that he has a habit of doing that."

"Oh," Slater mumbled, his voice flat.

Zack ran a hand back through his blond hair in frustration, then thrust the clipboard at his friend. "See if you can find a juggler anywhere in here, or a tumbling act, or a snake charmer."

Slater pushed the mass of paperwork back to Zack. "I don't have to look. I know Jessie well enough to know she wouldn't think of those things, so it's a good thing you're in charge now."

"You could be," Zack offered.

"The best man for the job has got the job," Slater insisted. "Besides, I'm the one who nominated you for it."

"Who seconded the motion?" Zack demanded, his eyes narrowed in suspicion.

Slater rubbed his jaw thoughtfully. "That's hard to say; there were so many relieved shouts of approval, I can't narrow it down to one person."

"Thanks," Zack growled, "but I think I could have done without such a vote of confidence. Do you know, I haven't had a chance to be with Kelly since early this morning? And I'm afraid I'll have to break our date for Friday night just to check in with all the committees." He sighed deeply. "And I was really looking forward to watching Jean-Pierre take on two dozen bad guys single-handedly."

"A Bonjour movie? Hey, if you can't go with Kel, I could always take your place," Slater offered.

Zack snarled at him.

"It was just a suggestion," Slater said.

"Then take another suggestion," Zack said. "Go find Sidney Tupperman and talk him into dressing like a clown, riding his unicycle, and selling balloons. Then flirt with Ula Tweedy until she promises to be a rubber woman."

"A what?" Slater demanded.

"You mean you never saw her bend backward until she looked like a human pretzel?" Zack asked. "Now that's a sight people would really be willing to shell out cash to see."

Chapter 8

▲ ▼ ▲ ▼ ▲

When the sun crested over the desert mountains east of Palisades the morning of the carnival, Zack felt as if he hadn't slept in days. Even when he had drifted off, it had been to dream of balloons, ponies, snake charmers, dunk tanks, and kissing booths, and each dream had had a Virtual Reality look to it.

As expected, he had ended up canceling his date with Kelly the night before, and was depressed over having done so. At least his dreams would have been far more pleasant if he'd spent a couple of hours watching Jean-Pierre kick sense into a bunch of bad guys, munching popcorn, and smelling Kelly's floral-scented perfume.

A sweet good-night kiss would have been nice, too.

One of the worst parts about ending up in charge of the carnival was that he had to be on the school grounds at eight o'clock on a Saturday morning. Wasn't it bad enough he had to be there that early weekdays? Zack wondered as he parked his car and gathered up his clipboard.

Because most of the booths had been set up the day before after school, Zack expected the carnival area to look like a ghost town. He doubted any teenager would tumble out of bed any earlier than necessary on a weekend, so he was surprised to find the area already a beehive of activity.

Over in the ride area, a long horse trailer was pulled up, and ponies were being led out of it. As he watched, Kelly came down the ramp leading a pure white pony by its halter. She spotted Zack and waved to him. He willed her to pass the pony's lead rope to another volunteer and run over to greet him, but Kelly turned her attention back to her uncle's animals.

Briefly Zack wondered if she was mad at him for breaking their date. But time to spend fretting about personal things was cut short when other carnival workers noticed his arrival and converged in a mass on him.

"When is the power going to be turned on at the stage? We can't do a sound check until . . ."

"Someone stole the center pole of the fortune-telling tent last night, and the roof is drooping. You've got to fix it, Zack, because . . ."

"We can't fill the dunk tank. The hose doesn't stretch that far and . . ."

"You've got to talk to Mac and the other jocks. They're supposed to be filling balloons with helium but they're breathing the gas themselves to make their voices sound silly. If someone doesn't get them back to work . . ."

Zack held up his hands, palms out. "Wait a minute."

The crowd actually hushed.

"Okay. Brad, you live only a couple blocks away, right? Dash home and borrow your dad's garden hose, and maybe the neighbor's, too. I want that tank filled by nine thirty so we can test it."

Brad saluted and took off running.

"The electricity will be turned on when Mr. Monza gets here at nine, so you'll have to be patient and test the sound system later, Greg. In the meantime, see if you can't help Phyllis with her tent."

Greg grumbled as he escorted Phyllis back to her booth, the many chains and bracelets of her gypsy costume jangling as they walked.

"Anybody see Slater?" Zack asked. "He can keep the football team from goofing off. Now, who else has a problem?"

There were lots of people who did, but Zack

managed to solve all their problems in time to make it to the dunk tank at exactly 9:30. Mr. Belding was already there, dressed in a pair of wildly colored Bermuda shorts, an even wilder-colored Hawaiian shirt, and sandals. Zack figured even Screech's weird wardrobe would pale next to the principal at the moment.

Mr. Belding clasped Zack on the shoulder. "You've done a fine job with this carnival, son," he said. "I'm proud of you, but a little confused. Although you were the one who presented the idea to me, I was under the impression that Jessie was going to run things."

"So was I, sir," Zack admitted, "but she got involved in practicing for a show."

"Well, I'm looking forward to seeing it and visiting every single one of the booths," Mr. Belding said. "I promised Mrs. Belding that we'd make a day of it here, and she's anxious to get started. Aren't you, dear?" he asked a pretty woman standing off to the side.

"Absolutely," she agreed.

Zack welcomed Mrs. Belding, then glanced into the tank of water. Garden hoses dangled over the side, still shooting steady streams of water into it, but the level was just about right for a test dunk, he figured.

Setting his clipboard aside, Zack signaled the principal. "I hope you're just as ready to get started as your wife is, sir. All you have to do is scramble up onto this seat and hope everyone who tries to dunk you has a bad throwing arm."

Mr. Belding chuckled. "Then I'm only in big trouble if members of the baseball team show up," he said.

"Or the football team, or the basketball team, or—"

"I'm lucky the tennis team is out of town, then," Mr. Belding said.

At least someone was happy about that, Zack thought. Lisa had been really ticked off that her boyfriend Keith would not be around to help her with the ponies.

"All settled?" Zack asked.

Mr. Belding nodded. "Ready. Who's going to try their hand first?"

"I am," Zack announced, and dug in his pocket for a dollar, handing it over to Alan Witkin in exchange for three softballs.

"Well, at least I know I'll stay nice and dry with this pitcher at the plate," Mr. Belding quipped. "Come on, Morris. Give it your best shot."

Zack wound up and pitched his first ball at the bright red target to the right of the tank. He hit it directly in the center, causing a bell to ring and the platform on which Mr. Belding was perched to tilt and pitch him into the water.

Everyone laughed, including Mrs. Belding.

"Lucky shot, Morris," the principal insisted, shaking water from his hair as he climbed back onto the platform. "You couldn't do that again in a million years."

Zack tossed his second ball. The bell sounded and Mr. Belding submerged again.

"Boy, does time ever fly," Zack mused as the dripping principal regained his seat. "That must have been the fastest million years in history."

"Why do I get the idea that you've been holding out on me, Zack? There's nothing in your file that indicates you ever tried out for baseball."

"You checked?"

"A person doesn't get to be principal without being thorough. Or careful," Mr. Belding said.

"I guess there was no mention of my sandlot baseball record," Zack said, winding up for his final throw. "I pitched eight no-hitter games out of ten, two years in a row."

"Now he tells me," Mr. Belding moaned before spilling into the water a third time.

▲　▼　▲

The longest line was at the cheerleaders' kissing booth. Some guys enjoyed their kiss then immediately got back in line again.

Kelly closed her eyes, kissed the guy before her quickly, and whisked the dollar out of his hand. "Have a nice day," she told him.

"I will now," he sighed, a goofy smile on his face.

"Next!" Kelly called.

"Hi, Kelly," a voice she hadn't heard in a long time said.

"Jeff!" Kelly greeted him happily. Thomas Jefferson Racine belonged to Palisades's founding family. He was cute, nice, and rich. Lisa had dated him for a while and not long ago he had helped the gang trick a girl who planned to sabotage their Save the Beach crusade.

"What are you doing here?" Kelly asked.

"My mother's on the school board," he said. "When I heard what you were planning and why, I had to come."

"Too bad Lisa isn't a cheerleader anymore," Kelly said. "You could buy a kiss from her."

"Can I buy one from you instead?" Jeff asked.

"Sure," Kelly told him. "Two if you want."

Jeff handed over his money and received his quick kisses.

"Before I go, let me introduce you to my cousin," Jeff said, indicating the handsome young man behind him in line. "Kelly Kapowski, meet Theodore Roosevelt Racine."

"Naturally everyone calls me Teddy," Theodore hastened to add. "As a relative of Jeff's, can I impose on you for two kisses as well?"

"It's all for a good cause," Kelly told him brightly. "Let's see the color of your money, Teddy."

As the day progressed, Kelly noticed that Teddy

was her most frequent customer. She figured he'd spent twenty dollars before lunchtime just getting kisses from her.

When he showed up as she was getting ready to take a break, Kelly shook her head in wonder. "Don't you have anything better to do, Teddy?"

"I can't think of anything better than being kissed by you, Kelly," he insisted.

She laughed. "With all the great things to do here? I don't think you've walked around and seen the other booths yet."

"That's true," Teddy admitted. "I preferred to stay where I felt welcome rather than roam around with Jeff and his friends."

"You'd be welcome at any of the booths," Kelly said.

"But it isn't much fun visiting them unless you're with someone special," he said.

"You should have brought a date," Kelly suggested.

"I would have if every girl I knew didn't live in Massachusetts," Teddy murmured.

"Oh," Kelly sighed. "I didn't realize you were visiting from the East Coast. Have you ever been to California before?"

"Not since Jeff and I were ten," he said. "Listen, if you ever get a break, would you mind touring the rest of the carnival with me?"

"Sure," Kelly said. "In fact, I was about to take time out to grab some lunch right now. Just wait until

I turn in the money I've collected, and we can go head toward the refreshment booths."

Teddy gave her a wide smile. "I'll wait as long as you want, Kelly. After all, as far as I'm concerned, you're the most beautiful sight I've seen since I arrived a week ago."

Kelly's eyes brightened at the compliment. It reminded her of the lovely things she'd overheard Duncan tell Jessie. She didn't believe the line, though. "Now, I know that's a fib," she insisted with a slight laugh, "because we've got really gorgeous sunsets."

"They pale in comparison to your beauty," Teddy murmured.

Even if it wasn't true, Kelly decided, it sure was neat to have such a good-looking guy make it sound as if it was. "I'll be right back," she told him, wondering if he gave lessons in the way to deliver romantic lines. If so, she was signing Zack up immediately.

▲   ▼   ▲

Zack stood out of sight behind his dart-toss booth, spraying the balloons for the backboard with a special solution. "You sure this will work?" he asked Screech, who was busy squirting another set of balloons.

"I hope so," Screech said, his voice breaking on the last word. "I developed it to coat my lab gloves so they wouldn't break. Latex was too expensive to use, so I mixed my own sealer solution."

"Which is guaranteed to keep the balloons from breaking? Even if a dart hits them?" Zack demanded.

Screech's forehead crinkled in thought. "But if the idea is to break the balloons, and no one can, how do they manage to win the stuffed animals that were donated as prizes?"

"They don't," Zack said. "At least not easily. I'll keep a few balloons free of the coating so that some of them will break. Only these won't."

"Then what are you going to do with those cuddly little toys?" Screech asked.

"Sell them," Zack announced. "Think about it, Screech. All the guys who come to this booth are trying to show off for their girlfriends. They say, 'Which prize do you like best, honey?' and the girl says"—Zack made his voice go high as he imitated a girl's voice—"'Oh, I just love that one,' and she points to her favorite. Well, with my system, there is very little chance of the dude breaking the three balloons he needs in order to win the stuffed animal. But he's determined to get it, right?"

"Right," Screech repeated, although he didn't look too clear on the idea.

"After a while his girlfriend gets bored and wanders off. That's when I tell him he can buy her the prize if he wants. Well, naturally, he'll jump at the chance and just tell her he won it. Either way, this booth makes a fortune," Zack finished.

"Is that fair?" Screech wondered.

"Fair, schmair," Zack said. "We're here to make money for the computer lab, and I plan to make this booth the one that takes in the most."

"Even more than the kissing booth?" Screech asked. "They've got pretty long lines over there. And I heard that one guy has spent a bundle just kissing Kelly."

Zack picked up a dart and stabbed at one of the newly coated balloons. The sharp tip bounced off it. "One of the nerds, huh?" he said.

"I don't think so, but he could be," Screech admitted. "He came with Jeff Racine, then just kept getting back in line for Kelly to kiss him."

Inside the booth they heard one of the volunteer workers talking to an eager contestant. A moment later the sound of a balloon breaking, then another, and another was heard.

Zack grinned. "Ah, a good excuse to replace the inferior balloons with these new, improved models," he said. "Thanks for sharing your formula with me, buddy. Now you'd better get back to the VR rides. How's it going over there, anyway?"

"Great," Screech said. "But we've got one customer who keeps coming back for more rides. It took three of us to get him to give up his visor the last time. I think he's getting addicted to VR."

"Whoa! We don't want that," Zack murmured. "I guess I'll have to talk to the guy and ban him from the ride. If that doesn't work, Slater and a couple of the other muscle-bound guys can just carry him away. Who is it anyway? Do I know him?"

Screech's mouth twisted in a funny-looking line. "I think so," he said. "It's Mr. Belding."

Chapter 9

▲ ▼ ▲ ▼ ▲

Slater stood to the back of the crowd watching as Jessie and Duncan Connor performed on the small stage. Rather than have a booth or tent, the magic show was given in a theater created by a clever placement of fabric-covered frames that served as walls. Before each show, Jessie and her magician stood outside the theater selling admission tickets. Duncan did card tricks to lure carnival goers into wanting to see the show and, judging by how packed the tiny theater was, sales were good.

So that Jessie wouldn't know he would be in the audience watching them, Slater had sent Butch Henderson over to buy a ticket for him, then had slipped away from the arm-wrestling booth just before the show started.

Jessie was the first to take the stage. She looked gorgeous, Slater thought. Her long curly hair was swept up and she was wearing the short pink sequined gown she'd worn when he'd taken her to the junior prom the year before.

"Ladies and gentlemen," she announced in a clear, bright voice, then swept her arm to stage left in a dramatic gesture. "Connor the Conjurer!"

There was a puff of smoke, and Duncan appeared next to her, his dark tuxedo, top hat, and silk-lined cape looking exotic and classy when compared to the shorts, jeans, and T-shirts worn by the audience.

Jessie took his cape, swirling it dramatically. As she laid it aside on a chair, Duncan took his hat off, acted as if he would pass it to her as well, then paused, tipped it over, and looked inside.

"Excuse me," he told the audience. "We have a slight problem. It won't take but a moment to clear up." He moved a step back on the stage, gesturing Jessie to follow him. "How many times have I asked you to keep your pets away from my things?" he said in an insistent whisper that carried to everyone in the audience.

Jessie peered inside his top hat. "Oh, dear!" she gasped. "How did you get in there?" There were giggles and sighs of "aah" when she reached inside and gathered up a white rabbit, cuddling him to her cheek.

As she moved to the side of the stage and bent to tuck the bunny into a wire cage, Duncan turned the hat over and tapped it, as if emptying it. Then he walked to the front of the stage.

"Sorry about that," he told the audience. "Empty now, though. See?" He held the hat so that everyone could see that there was nothing inside it. "You see any rabbit whiskers in there?" he asked a child in the front row.

When the kid peeped closer and then shook his head, Duncan looked relieved. He started to put the hat on the chair, then pulled it back.

"I thought you told me it was empty," he said to the child.

"It was," a small voice insisted.

"Then where did this come from?" He pulled another rabbit from the interior and held it out to Jessie. She'd barely cuddled it when Duncan made a face and lifted another rabbit out.

Each rabbit was smaller than the last, Slater noticed, but they were all pure white, a real contrast to Duncan's black tuxedo and the red silk on the inside of his top hat. When there were six different rabbits in the cage, Duncan looked relieved. This time he managed to put the hat down, but he'd barely turned away when a pure white dove fluttered out of it and perched on the back of the chair. Duncan looked really shocked to find his hat was now spewing birds. He picked it up, turned it to face the audience again, then punched his fist through it so that the crown hung open, like a little round door.

"That should fix it," Duncan insisted. But when he set the hat aside again, another dove hopped out.

The audience chuckled and clapped. When Duncan looked over at Jessie, she shrugged her shoulders and shook her head to indicate she had no idea where the birds were coming from.

Slater slipped out of the tent. He'd seen enough. He hadn't been looking at the magician's tricks, though. He'd been watching the way Jessie's eyes glowed when they met Duncan's.

She'd sure never looked at him that way when they were dating, he thought, disgruntled. Of course, they had usually been too busy arguing to exchange tender glances.

It had been a long time since they'd gone together, and it had been his idea to break up. He'd simply been tired of the way she managed to forget him and any plans they had made when she got interested in a project. Since then he'd dated a few girls but hadn't felt like getting to know them as well as he knew Jessie. She hadn't found a new boyfriend, either, and he had thought she was interested in getting back together with him.

Heck, Slater admitted to himself, he'd thought about it himself. But then he'd remember the arguments and the cavalier way Jessie had treated him, and he'd look around for another girl to take out, hoping she'd be special enough to make him forget Jessie.

Now it looked as if she had forgotten him. Replaced him with a guy who was not only good-looking, but, judging from what he'd seen of the magic show, talented. There was something about being in competition with a guy like that that depressed him.

If he could be called *in competition for Jessie*, that is. Slater had a feeling that she wouldn't even notice that he existed if he stood next to her. At the moment, Jessie only had eyes for Duncan Connor.

When it was his turn to arm wrestle with eager challengers, Slater pictured the magician as his opponent and quickly pinned each hapless contestant. After decimating a dozen of them, he still didn't feel any better.

▲   ▼   ▲

Teddy Racine gazed happily across the picnic table at Kelly as she tried to take a small, ladylike bite of a chili dog.

"You know, you would fit in so well at an eastern college, Kelly. Have you applied to any?" he asked.

She licked chili sauce from the corner of her mouth. "No, but not because I wouldn't love to go to one," she said. "It's just that I can't afford to move across the country or pay the tuition costs for out-of-state students. They are so high."

"Would you go if you had a scholarship?"

Kelly laughed softly. "You haven't seen my grade point average. If you had, you wouldn't even mention the word *scholarship.*"

"You should have seen my GPA," Teddy said. "I had two teachers congratulating me on making the lowest possible passing grade in their classes. My high school counselor told me there wasn't a college in the world that would let me in the door. But I'm in my second year at Massachusetts University."

"Massachusetts University?" Kelly echoed.

"MU is a small but excellent school," Teddy told her. "It's nestled in a beautiful valley. We've got acres of woods for hiking, a lake for boating, and a ski lodge barely an hour's drive away. All the major Greek sororities and fraternities have houses there, and our cricket team has traveled to Wimbledon to play the Oxford team."

Kelly blinked in surprise. "You have a cricket team?"

"We like to think we're ahead of everyone else when it comes to a diversity of sports," Teddy said modestly.

"Oh. But I thought they only played tennis at Wimbledon."

"Did I say Wimbledon? I meant Whimpledon," Teddy corrected hastily.

"What about academics? How does MU rank against other schools?" Kelly asked.

"Oh, at the top," Teddy assured her. "But the really great thing about MU is the great financial aid they offer to students. Because we have many successful businessmen and -women who are alumni who donate to the scholarship fund, we have scads of money that doesn't even get used each year."

"You're kidding!" Kelly said.

"I'd love it if you chose MU to be your school, but there are dozens of other colleges just as good in the East. And my family knows lots of people who can put in a good word for you so you can have a full scholarship anywhere you want to go," Teddy said.

Kelly finished her chili dog. "It all sounds too good to be true," she told him.

"All it takes is knowing someone," Teddy insisted. "And now that you know me, I can put you in touch with the right people."

"I don't know," Kelly murmured.

Teddy rested his arms on the table and leaned closer to her. "Have you ever been to New York City, Kelly?"

"Once," she said. "It was a school trip and—"

"How about Boston?"

"No, but—"

"Philadelphia?"

"No, however—"

"What about Niagara Falls?"

"No, I haven't, yet—"

"The Great Lakes?"

"I don't see what—"

"Kelly, Kelly, Kelly," Teddy murmured, shaking his head slowly. "You really haven't lived, have you?"

"Well, I'm only seventeen," she insisted. "I've got time."

"You just think you do," he said. "It goes by so fast. Why, before I know it, I'll be twenty-one, and it's all downhill from then on."

"It is?"

"Listen, you just say the word, and I'll place a couple of calls today and get the wheels moving for you. Why, in no time at all you'll be packing and on your way," Teddy assured her. "So, what do you say?"

Kelly glanced at her watch. "I say I should have been back at the kissing booth five minutes ago." She got to her feet.

So did Teddy. "There's nothing like a school on the opposite side of the country from your parents, Kelly. Believe me. I know. Let me make those calls."

"Really, Teddy. It's so sudden. I have to think." She glanced at her watch again. "And I have to go. See you."

As she dashed through the crowd back to the

cheerleaders' booth, Kelly wondered what it would be like to go to school on the Atlantic seaboard. Did MU have a drama department? She should have asked Teddy. Of course, since she wanted to be an actress, it would be convenient to be near New York. There were all those Broadway and Off-Broadway plays to see. And, of course, she knew people in New York City. True, they were really Mitch Tobias's friends, but she was sure he'd put in a good word for her with them if need be. Maybe Mitch knew something about Massachusetts University. She could call him and . . .

Kelly realized that she had dropped to a slow walk and was going to be even later getting back from her lunch break. Pushing thoughts of college out of her mind, she ran the rest of the way to the booth.

▲   ▼   ▲

Screech helped Mrs. Belding escort her husband away from the Virtual Reality ride area.

"There has to be some mistake," Mr. Belding insisted as they hustled him out of line and down the aisle of carnival booths. "I'm a principal, not a troublemaker. As long as I can pay the admission price, I should be allowed to ride the VR roller coaster as much as I want."

Mrs. Belding frowned at him. "You were sick after your last ride, Richard."

"So would you be after doing a three-hundred-sixty-degree double loop-the-loop," he said. "But the really great thing is that while you're hanging upside down, you aren't really hanging upside down. You just think you are."

"I forbid you to go on that ride again, Richard," Mrs. Belding said sternly.

"And Zack said he'd send the football team over to tackle you if you tried to take one of the visors by force again," Screech said.

Mr. Belding looked sullen. "All I wanted to do was have some fun," he mumbled.

"I think you've had just about enough fun for the day," Mrs. Belding insisted. "Thank you, Samuel. I think I can handle things from here. Go back to your friends."

Screech watched as she guided the principal through the parking lot to their car before he turned back to the carnival.

Not far away, Sidney Tupperman rocked his unicycle back and forth to keep his balance, his large clown shoes flapping with the motion. He held a group of brightly colored balloons in one hand and was trying to make change for a father who had just bought his child a balloon.

Briefly Screech considered getting a unicycle of his own, then remembered how long he had kept the training wheels on his bicycle. He was probably better off sticking to inventing things. Of course, he could always create a robot who used a unicycle-like wheel system to get around. The robot would have a gyro system to keep its balance, something he seemed to be missing in his own genetic makeup.

While Screech mused, Sidney completed his sale and started to pedal off. Just then a bunch of rowdy kids ran by and stuck the child's balloon and those that Sidney held, causing them all to break with loud pops. When the child began crying, the hoodlums laughed and ran away.

Sidney looked as if he wanted to cry, too, but was fighting back tears because they would make his clown makeup run. The father looked both angry and helpless as he tried to comfort his child.

Screech dashed up to them and knelt down by the weeping kid. "Don't worry. I'll go get you another one," he promised. "What color do you want?"

"Boo," the tyke said with a sniffle.

"Blue," Screech repeated. "You stay right here, okay?" He looked to the child's father, waiting for the man's nod of approval as well before getting back to his feet.

Sidney got off his unicycle, clown feet slapping the ground with each step he took. "That's the third time that bunch of creeps broke all my balloons," he said. "They're trying to ruin this carnival."

"I should have known better than to buy one," the father said. "I saw those kids earlier taking great pleasure in popping other balloons."

Screech got a determined look on his face. "Well,

they won't break any more of them today," he said through clenched teeth. "I'll see to that."

When he returned five minutes later, the balloons he handed to Sidney and presented to the child had been treated with his special puncture-proof solution.

Chapter 10

▲ ▼ ▲ ▼ ▲

Lisa poked one finger against the pony's flank, trying to get it moving without actually touching it for long. "Come on, move," she urged.

The pony looked back at her as if to ask if she was serious, but it didn't stir.

Atop the saddle, a little boy bounced in his seat. "Giddap," he shouted. "Giddap, giddap."

His high-pitched yell was enough to give Lisa a headache.

"Perhaps the animal would move if you pulled on the bridle," the tyke's mother suggested.

Lisa glanced at the pony's bridle. Its teeth were awfully close to where the woman wanted her to put her hand. Of course, Kelly's cousins had led the ponies that way, and they hadn't been bitten. But they also hadn't just had their nails done, Lisa thought. Nor had they been dressed in a midriff-skimming top, shorts, and flimsy sandals as she was. They had worn long-sleeved western shirts, jeans, and heavy cowboy boots.

Lisa looked the pony in the eyes and was sure it rolled its lip, allowing her a better view of big, slightly yellow teeth. She could almost see it trying to decide if it would be more fun to take a bite out of her or just tromp on her.

"Ah," Lisa began.

A large masculine hand reached past her and took hold of the pony's bridle. "Here you go, bucka-roo," Jeff Racine said to the bouncing boy on the animal's back.

"Yahoo!" the child yelled.

Lisa winced at his volume.

"How many times do we go around the circle, Lisa?" Jeff asked as he started walking around the pony track.

"Four," Lisa said.

"Five," the child's mother reminded. "It says five on the sign."

Lisa sighed and rubbed her forehead. "Five, Jeff. Thank you for helping out."

"No problem," he called. "What happened to the helpers you had earlier?"

"They called a lunch break," she answered. "Can

you believe it? And if that isn't bad enough, they suggested I water the ponies and unsaddle a couple of them while they were gone."

"They obviously didn't know who they were dealing with," Jeff said, hiding a grin as he led the pony back around the small track a second time.

"To top it all off, I've had to put up with this horrible smell all day," she complained. "I've used up a whole bottle of perfume trying to get rid of it. I've sprayed the air, the ponies, the saddles—"

"I'll bet the owner loved that," Jeff murmured as if commiserating with her.

"He got pretty red in the face," Lisa admitted. "Then he stormed off, telling his kids that he'd be back when it was time to load everything back into the trailer. He might be Kelly's uncle, but he sure isn't anything like her."

"Are you having fun, Petey?" the woman called to her son.

"Faster," Petey cried, and bounced harder, kicking his heels against the saddle.

"Whoa, partner," Jeff said when the child started to slip from his seat. "This is the Bayside carnival, not the Bayside rodeo."

The boy pouted, sticking his bottom lip out.

A few minutes later, the five laps were completed and Petey and his mother were on their way to the cotton candy stand. Lisa hastily scrawled a sign that claimed the booth was closed for lunch, and sank with a sigh into a chair in the shade.

"Thank you for rescuing me, Jeff," she said. "I knew it was a mistake to get stuck with the ponies, but I couldn't find anybody else to take my place."

"My pleasure," he told her. "It isn't often I get to play Sir Galahad to a damsel in distress. Although, in a way, that's what I was doing in looking for you."

Lisa brightened. "Really? You were looking for a girl to rescue, and I got to be her?"

"Well, not exactly," Jeff said. "It was your friend Kelly I was going to rescue. If she needed rescuing, that is."

"Kelly? I don't think Zack would like you doing anything for her. They're going steady, you know."

"I just want to warn her," Jeff explained. "You see, I brought my cousin Teddy along with me today, and he's been hanging around her a lot."

Lisa frowned, her headache forgotten. "What do you mean, warn her? Warn her about what? Is he dangerous?"

"No. He's just . . . well, eager to please. The trouble is, if necessary, he'll make things up to impress someone. Volunteer to do things for people, especially girls, that he can't really do."

Lisa gaped at him. "He lies to girls?"

"Yes, but he's very charming as he does it," Jeff insisted. "Or, at least, his mother claims he is. We're all hoping Teddy grows out of his need to please people so much. In the meantime, it might be a good idea to hint to Kelly that she shouldn't believe everything Teddy tells her."

Lisa sighed deeply. "You know," she said, "this is quickly becoming the worst day of my life."

Jeff grinned and patted her hand. "Come now. It could be lots worse, Lisa. Teddy could have been feeding his charming lies to you."

▲   ▼   ▲

Jessie waited until Duncan had fed and watered the rabbits and doves before handing him the cola she'd bought from a nearby refreshment booth.

He grinned at her before taking a long, welcome swallow. "You are not only intelligent and beautiful, you are a true lifesaver," he insisted. "Do you know, as fantastic as southern California is, it has definite drawbacks. Like weather that is far too warm to make a guy in a tuxedo feel comfortable. Especially when he spends most of his time standing in the sun."

"Poor Duncan," Jessie soothed. "But it isn't for much longer. When the carnival closes in an hour, you can change and we can do something to cool off."

"That sounds like you have a plan, Ms. Spano," Duncan said, taking another gulp of icy cola.

"I might, Mr. Connor," Jessie teased. "The weather forecaster says the moon will be bright and the tide will be out. That means conditions for night swimming are perfect."

Duncan finished his drink and crumpled the cup. He pitched it toward a trash container.

From the shade of a nearby tent, Slater watched as the cup flew straight into the basket.

"Two points," Duncan murmured, then slipped his arms around Jessie's waist. "A moonlit swim, hmm? Sounds dangerous."

Jessie slipped her arms around his neck. "Don't worry. As long as we stay in the shallows together, we'll be fine."

"And if I get a cramp and need saving?" Duncan teased.

"Then I'll save you," Jessie said. "And if need be, I'll even give you CPR."

"Mouth-to-mouth?" Duncan asked softly. "I like the sound of that even better."

Jessie smiled gently. "I'm a little out of practice. Perhaps I should brush up a bit."

When she leaned forward to kiss the magician, Slater ground his teeth together and slipped away rather than torture himself with Jessie's happiness.

Jessie was definitely out of his life now. There was no doubt in his mind that she was in love with Duncan Connor. Slater decided he didn't want to know if the magician was in love with her, too. The guy was perfect for her. He was tall, handsome, intelligent, charming, and planning on becoming a lawyer. If he was working in Kenyon Sinclair's office, he was probably even involved in the same ecological and historical preservation projects that Jessie's future stepfather advocated.

Next to Duncan Connor, A. C. Slater was nothing more than a memory. A pleasant one, he hoped.

Well, there was only one thing to do to help him forget Jessie, and that was to find himself a new girlfriend. There were hundreds of possible candidates roaming the carnival grounds. Many had already tossed welcoming smiles his way that day. Since his shift at the arm-wrestling booth was over, there was nothing to stop him from immediately setting out in search of a gorgeous girl of his own.

Instead of going off to flirt with anyone, though, Slater headed for Zack's dart-throwing booth.

▲   ▼   ▲

Zack leaned up against the counter and watched as Slater aimed a dart with precision and let it fly. It hit the rounded curve of a red balloon and bounded off, sticking straight into the ground.

"Ah, too bad," Zack commiserated. "Want another try?"

Slater frowned. "I've already spent five dollars and haven't popped a single balloon."

"That's the breaks," Zack said. "Or rather, it isn't."

"But I've hit every balloon," Slater pointed out.

"You aren't the only guy to tell me that," Zack murmured. "But you know, I've got a theory about why they aren't breaking."

"Which is?" Slater asked.

"Well, don't laugh, but whenever these balloons see a sharp-tipped dart headed toward them, determined to break 'em, they concentrate real hard and will it to fail."

"Is that so?" Slater growled.

"Hey! I've seen it happen time and again today," Zack insisted.

"So how come the pile of stuffed animals you had earlier is nearly gone?" Slater demanded.

"Just shows that some guys are more patient than you are at this game," Zack said.

"It wouldn't have anything to do with that spray Screech has been squirting on balloons?" Slater asked.

Zack faked a surprised look. "Screech has got a special spray?" he gasped. "What's it do?"

"Makes balloons unbreakable. Sorta like these are." Slater picked up another dart and pitched it. The targeted yellow balloon thought really hard, and managed to repel the dart on impact.

"That," Zack announced, "will cost you another dollar."

Lisa dragged up to the counter as Slater handed over his money and received another two darts.

"I am exhausted," she announced.

"You're rather fragrant, too," Slater said, wrinkling his nose as he moved away from her.

"It's those darn ponies," Lisa moaned. "They smell horribly!"

"Since when did ponies start smelling like Screech did the day he knocked into the perfume model at the mall and got a whole bottle of cologne spilled on him?" Slater asked.

Lisa sighed deeply. "Hey, all I did was squirt a few drops of Essence of Island Jungle around to improve the milieu."

Screech sidled up to the booth. "You do kitten imitations, Lisa? Neat! Was that a Persian or a Siamese?"

"It was French, dork," Lisa growled.

Screech frowned in thought. "French? I didn't know they had their own breed of cat. It was definitely not mentioned in my Encyclopedia Knowitallitus CD-ROM. I must call the omission to their attention."

Lisa let out a muffled scream of frustration.

"Having a bad day, Lise?" Zack asked.

"Incredibly," she snarled.

Slater handed her his darts. "Here. Exercise your anger away."

"It won't help," Lisa insisted, but she did take a

dart and throw it at the balloons attached to the board at the back of the booth. It sailed straight into a purple one, popping it with a loud bang.

"See," Zack said to Slater. "You just weren't using the right technique."

Lisa sighed gustily. "You know, I do feel better," she declared, and handed the last dart back to Slater. "Thanks."

"So what's gone wrong for you today, Lise?" Zack asked.

"You name it. It was bad enough that Keith couldn't be here to help me, but then Kelly's bratty cousins abandoned me with those horrible ponies, and Jeff came by, but he was more interested in rescuing Kelly, and—"

Zack jerked out of his slouched stance. "What did you say about Kelly?"

"She's got the world's nastiest cousins," Lisa said.

"No, after that."

"Umm. Oh, that Jeff wanted to rescue her."

"Jeff Racine?" Zack demanded.

"It wouldn't be so irritating if it was somebody else named Jeff," Lisa said. "But it is *very* irritating to have an old boyfriend saying he was playing Sir Galahad to another girl. Who is Sir Galahad, anyway?"

"He's my favorite knight," Screech announced.

"Friday's mine," Slater said. "It always gets my weekend off to a good start."

Zack drummed his fingers on the counter. "Why did Jeff want to rescue Kelly?"

Lisa leaned weakly against the booth. "Something about being afraid his cousin would tell her lies or something. Jeez, do you realize how many crummy cousins are at this carnival today? The place is crawling with them."

Zack cleared his throat. "Lisa?"

"Oh yeah. It seems that Jeff's cousin Teddy likes to make people happy, so he tells them what he thinks they'd like to hear. Well, I would have come right over here and told you, but I was chained to that stupid pony ride. Besides, the more I thought about it, the more I realized that Kelly wouldn't pay any attention to the guy because she's going steady with you," Lisa explained. "It doesn't matter that Teddy didn't visit any booth but the cheerleaders' one. He must have spent a fortune because he was always in line to kiss her."

"*He what?*" Zack snapped, his eyes nearly starting from his head.

"Lots of guys were doing that, Zack," Lisa said with a casual, unconcerned shrug.

Zack wasn't listening, though. He vaulted over the counter. "Take over," he snarled over his shoulder to Slater. "I'll be right back."

Slater shook his head slowly as he watched Zack stride away. "Nice going, Lisa."

Lisa stared after Zack, but she was smiling as she did so. "I think so, too," she agreed contentedly. "Hey, can I have more of those darts? This is kind of fun."

Chapter 11

▲ ▼ ▲ ▼ ▲

Zack stalked through the crowd of carnival-goers, not even aware that many turned to look at him in surprise when he plowed past them without returning their calls of greeting.

He couldn't believe it. Here he'd gone to a bunch of trouble to make Kelly fall back in love with him and agree to go steady with him, and the minute he got swamped with responsibilities, some other guy tried to steal her away.

A guy he didn't even know.

That made him a little nervous. After all, look how nuts Slater was acting over Jessie and the magician. A fellow usually knew where he stood with a girl when the other guy trying to worm his way into her life was someone they'd both grown up with. But when the competition was a stranger, it was harder to convince yourself that you were the better man, Zack thought uneasily.

It was good to know someone really well, but that also meant you knew their faults really well, too. And, boy, did Kelly know his!

She hated it when he scammed, so he'd been trying to stop. Which was really hard, considering he had worked so hard over the years to perfect his technique. He'd always been proud to be known as the scammeister. But if Kelly wanted him to change, he'd try to change.

Of course, there were situations when she wanted him to use his abilities. Like when Lisa and Screech had needed to find out that the surfers they'd been spending time with weren't really interested in them. They'd just wanted to ensure the gang lost the volleyball game at the Save the Beach festival. Kelly had been all for a scam that time. She'd even run a scam of her own, talking other surfers on the team into puting on a strenuous surfing exhibition just before the game so that they'd be tired.

He'd been really proud of her, although he'd been really jealous and hurt before he found out she'd been flirting with the big, handsome dudes for a specific reason. The shoe had been on the other foot that day. It had always been him doing the flirting in the past. But the days of looking at other girls were over. From now on Kelly was the only one for him.

At least she was if she hadn't gotten interested in another guy while he was busy with the school carnival. After all, he had backed out on his date with her the night before, Zack reminded himself.

It was going to take some pretty fancy footwork to make her forgive him for that. She probably thought that the carnival had just been an excuse, that he was really out with another girl.

Not that he could blame Kelly. He'd lied about what he was doing a lot of times so that he could date other girls. There had been so many now, he'd almost lost count. None of them had meant as much to him as Kelly did. He'd been in love with her forever, and figured he probably would always be.

What he needed to do was something so heroic and romantic that she'd fall into his arms, her blue eyes glowing with love, and swear she'd never even think of dating another guy again.

Zack reached the pony rides. He remembered how Kelly had looked as she led the white pony from the horse trailer that morning, her long dark hair blowing softly in the wind, a happy smile curving her lips.

In his mind's eye, Kelly was no longer wearing jeans and a T-shirt, but a long, flowing dress. Instead of balloons and banners, the carnival grounds suddenly sported colorful pennants and brightly colored striped tents with still more pennants snapping in the wind. The families disappeared, replaced by more girls in long dresses and guys in shiny armor.

His armor was mirror bright, gleaming in the sun. The feathery plume on his helmet was golden and nearly as perfect as his blond hair, Zack mused, enjoying the mental picture. He was mounted on the pure white pony, and the crowd cheered him as he rode through it, intent upon reaching Kelly.

But such was not to be the case. Another knight rode up on a black pony, his armor inky as night, his intent even darker. He swept down on Kelly, swooped her up before him on the saddle, and galloped off.

Furious at the villain's deed, Zack urged his pony in pursuit. Soon they caught up with the black knight. "Put my girl down!" Zack ordered in a loud voice.

"*Your* girl? Ha!" the villain shouted. "She was just standing there waiting for a guy like me to come along. If you cared for her, you would have been at her side."

"I was busy," Zack growled.

"Doing what? Combing your hair? Practicing your smile?" the dark knight taunted.

"Doesn't everyone?" Zack zinged back coolly. "Unhand Kelly this minute."

"Ha! Make me!" the villain insisted, and stuck his tongue out at Zack.

"That does it!" Zack snarled, and, riding up to the other guy, he forked two fingers at him, waving them before the villain's eyes.

"You think I'll let you poke me?" The black knight laughed. He put his hand up sideways over his nose, blocking Zack's attempted attack.

Except that it was a fake attack. While the bad knight was busy protecting his eyes, Zack buffeted him on the shoulder, knocking him from the back of his black pony.

In the same instant, Zack swept Kelly onto his own pony and spurred his mount into a quick get-away.

"My hero!" Kelly sighed, cuddling in his arms.

"Always, my darling," Zack declared. He leaned forward in the saddle to kiss her and came out of his dream just before he stuck his nose into the sticky cloud of a little girl's cotton candy.

"Woops. Sorry," he said, and hustled off to the cheerleaders' kissing booth.

But when he got there he was in for a big shock. Kelly wasn't anywhere in sight!

"Hi, Zack!" Daisy Tyler greeted him. "Looking for Kelly? She just left with a really good-looking guy."

"Boy, was he," another of the cheerleaders sighed. "I just love guys who wear black silk shirts, don't you?"

Zack ground his teeth. The black knight had

beaten him out again! Well, it would be the last time that villain waltzed off with another guy's girl.

"Which way did they go?" he asked.

Daisy and the other girl pointed.

Directly at the fun house.

▲   ▼   ▲

It was kind of dark in the fun house, which made it spooky. Kelly hadn't seen much of the vampire who sat up in his coffin as they passed, or done much more than duck as a wispy ghost had swooped down. Her mind was still spinning over the option Teddy had offered her about scholarships to Massachusetts University.

To a girl who came from a large family and wasn't a brain like Jessie, the chance of getting a scholarship was more than welcome. She would be stupid to give it up.

Yet the idea of moving so far away bothered her. She was fond of her little brother and younger sisters and would miss them terribly. And since Zack hadn't decided what college he would attend next year, she couldn't even argue that in going to MU she would be close to him.

After all the time and energy she had put into their relationship, she didn't want to lose him by making it too easy for him to forget her. She knew too well that there were a lot of other girls who would jump at the opportunity to cheer him up after she left.

Kelly gritted her teeth together. Well, she wasn't going to let that happen.

Teddy reached for her hand and pulled her to stand with him before a looking glass in the hall of mirrors. He grinned happily at their reflection. "Hey, we make a pretty good-looking couple, don't we?"

Ew, Kelly thought. She really hated to hurt anybody's feelings, but it was time to give Teddy her decision.

"I can't go to MU, Teddy," she said softly.

He turned to face her. "You have to," he said. "I'll be desolate if you don't."

"You're very sweet, but my life isn't in the East. I have a family and a boyfriend here."

Teddy sighed and dropped his head, his chin resting on his chest. "Well, it was worth a shot," he murmured. "You're a very beautiful girl, Kelly. It would have been great to have you on my arm as I showed you around campus."

"Thank you, but I'm sure you have many other girls at MU who would be proud to be on your arm, Teddy."

"Not as many as I'd like," he told her with a small laugh. "At least you've made my visit a little happier. I've never spent so much money at one booth at a carnival before."

Kelly smiled gently. "The Bayside computer lab thanks you for your generosity," she said.

"I wasn't shelling out cash with your computer

lab in mind," Teddy confessed. "It was for the pure pleasure of having you kiss me."

Kelly went up on her toes and placed a kiss on his cheek. "Thank you anyway."

Teddy looked down at his feet. "I know this sounds terribly flaky, but would you mind if I left you here, Kelly? I think it's time I found Jeff and headed back home."

"I don't mind," she said. "Have a good flight back to MU."

He squeezed her hand. "I will." Then he turned and walked way, his image briefly reflected in all the mirrors before it disappeared.

▲   ▼   ▲

Zack tried to dash inside the fun house but was stopped by a vigilant Tony Berlando. "Where do you think you're going, Morris?" he asked, one strong hand landing on Zack's shoulder and bringing him to a jerking halt.

"I'm not going in here to enjoy myself," Zack insisted. "I'm looking for Kelly Kapowski."

"Whether you enjoy yourself or not, you've got to pay to get inside," Tony said.

"But I—"

"A buck, Morris," Tony reminded him.

Zack fished in his pocket and handed the admission price over.

"Thanks," Tony said, releasing Zack to place the dollar in his cash box. "Have fun."

Oh, he'd have fun, all right, Zack snarled to himself silently. He was on a crusade to win his girl back.

He had to stop inside the doorway to let his eyes adjust to the darkness. There were a lot of giggles and some squeals of delighted fright ahead of him in the dim light. Briefly he felt a sense of pride. He had been the one to come up with the ideas for the fun house, even if it had been Tony and some of his friends who had done the actual work.

They'd done a good job, too, Zack admitted, moving forward. Although he knew they were fake, he shivered a bit as he brushed through the curtain of cobwebs and felt the floor drop away in a steep incline. The sound of water lapping against something and the sound of a foghorn greeted him before a ghostly hand descended from the ceiling and grazed his head. Zack ducked and moved deeper into the gloom.

He thought he heard Kelly's voice over the other sounds in the fun house. He couldn't be sure because, if he was hearing right, she was doing cow imitations. There was a mumble of conversation and then Kelly's voice clearly saying "moo." It was very puzzling, especially since she kept saying it.

Zack followed the mooing sounds, hoping he was getting closer to where she was. Because of the dim lighting, he couldn't move at more than a snail's pace. He'd probably trip over one of the cleverly hidden props and break his leg if he rushed. The next time he suggested a fun house, he was going to demand a map so that in emergencies like this he could cut directly across the room instead of following the twisting path the workers had built.

Out of the dark, Kelly's voice rose in a shriek that had nothing to do with the spooky fun house entertainments. Zack threw caution to the winds and dashed forward to her rescue.

Chapter 12

▲ ▼ ▲ ▼ ▲

Kelly stood listening to Teddy's footsteps as they receded into the distance. She could hear a group of kids giggling and screaming as they worked their way through the fun house and told herself that she should be on her way back to the kissing booth, but she didn't move.

In a way she felt bad for disappointing Teddy, but on the other hand she felt good for turning down his offer. It was one thing, she thought, to accept favors from guys she knew, but to do so from ones who were strangers, no matter how handsome and charming, was another. Not a good idea in the least. Who knew what would be expected in return? What if she had let Teddy make those calls, had gotten a scholarship to MU or another eastern school, and then found he expected her to be his girlfriend in return for the favor? It would have been horrible! Not that she hadn't liked Jeff's cousin, but she knew nothing about him. When it came to serious dating, it was always better to know your date really well.

Like she knew Zack.

At the thought of him, her spirits rose and she smiled at her reflection in the mirror. It was distorted, giving her a tiny little body and a giant head.

"That's what you would look like if you had a really mega ego," she told herself with a little giggle. "But now you'd better get back to work at the booth." Funny the way kissing guys had proved to be really wearing work!

As she turned to follow the path, the bunch of noisy kids rushed around a corner and ran past her, screeching at something. One of them knocked into her, throwing her off balance. Kelly screamed shortly as she fell toward the mirrors, and managed to twist away from them, landing hard on the floor. That's all she needed, she thought. If one mirror had fallen and broken, the others would have followed like tumbling dominoes and she would have had seven years' bad luck times—how many mirrors were there? Ten! That was seventy years!

Zack skidded to a halt and dropped to his knees at her side. "Kelly! Are you all right? I was so worried! I heard this weird mooing and then you screamed and I—"

"Oh, Zack," she murmured, and hugged him tight. "You came to my rescue?"

"I'll always come to your rescue," he promised.

Kelly smiled happily. Oh yes, she told herself. She'd made the right decision. There might be easily won scholarships available elsewhere, but she would never have been happy if Zack weren't with her.

"Are you hurt? Can you stand?" he asked, his voice tight with concern.

"I'm fine," Kelly said.

"You've had a fright," he insisted. "You need to take it easy."

Kelly was surprised, and delighted, when he scooped her up in his arms and carried her out of the fun house.

▲   ▼   ▲

Lisa dabbed at her eyes with a tissue. "Oh, that is so romantic," she said with a wistful sigh.

"What is?" Slater asked. Despite the success of the arm-wrestling booth, he didn't look happy.

"That," Lisa said, pointing to where Zack had just exited the fun house, Kelly in his arms. She had linked her hands behind his neck and was resting her head on his shoulder.

Beside Lisa, Screech sighed as well. "It sure is," he agreed, and sniffled a bit. "They look just like the prince and princess in a fairy tale."

"If only a guy would be that romantic with me,"

Lisa murmured dreamily, "I'd probably fall madly in love with him on the instant."

"You would?" Screech demanded.

Before she realized what he was doing, Screech tried to sweep Lisa up in his arms. He'd barely picked her up when his knees wobbled and his legs collapsed. They ended in a pile on the ground, Lisa scrambling hastily to get away from him.

"What is with you, dork?" she demanded. "Are you trying to kill me?"

"I was only performing an act of love, my darling," Screech insisted.

"An act of stupidity, you mean," Lisa said. "Lay one more finger on me, and I'll break it."

"Ouch!" Screech murmured, just thinking about the possibility.

Lisa dusted dirt from her clothes. "Well, I think my work here is done," she said. "I've endured those stupid ponies, a bunch of noisy brats, and set Zack and Kelly back on the path of true love."

"I didn't know they were off it," Slater said.

"Trust me, sweetie, they were. It is much easier to be romantic when you aren't going steady, you know. You work harder to impress the other person. I've seen it happen a lot, which is why I've never gone steady with anyone myself," Lisa explained.

"I thought you were with Keith," Slater mumbled, a bit confused.

"It might look like that, but he hasn't officially

asked me, and I haven't officially accepted his letter sweater or school ring," Lisa pointed out. "Those are the things that make it official."

"So, if Keith asked you to go steady, you'd say no?" Slater asked.

Lisa chewed her lip in thought. "I don't know. It wouldn't be an easy decision to make, that's for sure. But I don't want to give up romance just to have a steady boyfriend."

Slater gazed after Zack and Kelly. "Is that what all girls want?"

"Absolutely," Lisa insisted. "Romance makes a girl feel really special, and that's super important."

"Hmm." Slater pondered a moment more before asking, "Would you teach me to be more romantic, Lisa? Tell me what girls like a guy to do?"

Lisa's eyes brightened. "There's someone you want to sweep off her feet?" she demanded, enthralled with the idea of being his romance counselor.

Thinking about how Jessie had looked in Duncan Connor's arms, Slater only shrugged. It wouldn't do for Lisa to know who he wanted to impress. "I just want to know for the future," he said. "When that special girl walks into my life, I don't want her to keep on walking because I don't know how to be romantic."

"You got it, sweetie. With my help, you'll turn into the most romantic guy in Bayside history," Lisa promised before looking serious again. "Oh, but, Slater? Once you've learned about this stuff, would you mind doing me a favor?"

"Anything, Lise," Slater said. "What is it?"

"Could you sort of drop hints to Keith?" Lisa asked. "I mean, he's gorgeous and loves me and all that, but the boy is in sad need of romantic guidance."

▲ ▼ ▲

On Monday morning, Mr. Belding called another schoolwide assembly. This time he looked much cheerier than he had the week before.

"I have some wonderful news for you," he announced. "Thanks to the terrific efforts of all of you, especially the senior class, we not only have sufficient money now to buy a few new computers, and the materials to fix the others, but we will also be able to hire technicians to help Mr. Monza and Mr. Hayes finish all the repairs within a month's time."

There were whistles, shouts, and a great deal of applause.

When the noise died down, Mr. Belding stepped back up to the microphone. "This means that the study halls that replaced the computer classes are canceled—"

There were even more whistles, shouts, and stomping of happy feet.

"Now, now. Those of you in those classes will still

be meeting in the cafeteria for the next month," the principal said.

Groans replaced the shouts.

"Thanks to the donations of some local businesses, we will be gaining new software for the computers, and you'll be spending the next weeks getting familiar with the instruction books."

"Cool!" Screech yelled. "I wonder what we're getting."

"I guess it's too much to hope that it's a copy of Mutant Alien Space Buddies?" Zack said.

"Far too much," Slater told him.

"Isn't it great?" Kelly gushed. "We actually did something really successful."

"And in an incredibly short time," Jessie added.

"I guess we'll all be graduating this year," Lisa said. "At least that's a relief."

"It sure is," Kelly agreed.

Mr. Belding took a sheet of paper from the inside pocket of his suit jacket. "While you all did a tremendous job, there are some people who deserve to be honored in particular for making this carnival such a success. The cheerleaders took in the most money at their kissing booth. While I can say I visited nearly all the booths personally on Saturday, I'm afraid Mrs. Belding wouldn't let me visit that one."

Laughter rippled through the room.

"Congratulations, ladies," Mr. Belding said. "We also need to thank Ms. Meadows for supervising the food booths, and not arguing too much over the addition of hot dogs and ice cream to the menu."

Slater turned to Zack. "I still don't know how you managed that one. Ms. Meadows is nearly as inflexible as Jessie is when it comes to food that is healthy to eat."

"I am not inflexible," Jessie said. "It just so happens, I've eaten peanut butter and jelly a few times."

"Keeping the new boyfriend happy, huh?" Slater sneered.

"You'd like Duncan if you took the time to get to know him," she insisted.

"I know I like him," Screech said. "How could you not like a guy who can make cute little bunnies appear just like that!" He tried to snap his fingers and failed.

"Perhaps our biggest thanks should be given to Jessie Spano for coming up with the idea for this carnival," Mr. Belding continued.

Zack's mouth dropped open. "Jessie!" he gasped as the assembly room echoed with new cheers.

"She did suggest it," Kelly said.

"But who did all the work?"

"Everyone," Lisa told him. "Some of us went beyond the call of duty, too. I can still smell those horrid ponies."

"But . . . but . . . ," Zack sputtered.

"And last, but not least, there is Zack Morris," the principal announced. "You did a fine job of taking on the job as CEO of this carnival, Zack. You surprised me, and I'm quite proud of you."

Zack relaxed and smiled as the students chanted his name.

"However," Mr. Belding said, "after the assembly there is something I'd like to talk to you about, Zack."

"Uh-oh," Slater murmured.

"What do you think Mr. B.'s talking about?" Jessie asked.

Zack looked at Screech. "I think I have an idea."

Screech had the grace to look uncomfortable.

The students were dismissed a few minutes later. Rather than head directly home as most of the school was doing, the gang trailed Zack to Mr. Belding's office.

The principal was standing outside the door, waiting for them.

"Ah, Morris. The man of the hour," he said.

Zack didn't think the look in the principal's eyes boded well for him.

"You really did a fine job this weekend, Zack," Mr. Belding said, "but there were some areas in which you really excelled."

Zack swallowed loudly. "There were? Any in particular, sir?"

"Now that you mention it, yes," Mr. Belding murmured, and reached over to open the door to his office. A cascade of balloons fell out of the room.

"I hope you have a way to deflate these," the

principal continued. "It seems that no matter what Mr. Monza and I stick them with, nothing will break them. You wouldn't happen to have had something to do with this phenomenon, would you?"

Zack gulped. "Ah . . ."

"That's what I thought," Mr. Belding said. "See what you can do, because if I don't have my office back very soon . . ."

"Gotcha," Zack assured, cutting the principal off before he could utter the dreaded word *detention*.

Zack turned quickly to his friends for help, but found they had all melted away, leaving him alone with the impossible chore.

"Morris?"

Zack sighed deeply. "Yes, sir. Right away," he said, and saluted. He waded through the balloons, feeling them close in behind him, hiding him from Mr. Belding's sight.

"Morris? Zack? Are you okay?" the principal asked.

"Fine," Zack called back, slipping to the window and easing it open. A moment later he'd thrown his leg over the sill and slipped away.

Behind him balloons escaped one at a time from the open window until they looked like colorful confetti all around the school yard.